SHADOWS BEHIND A SCREEN

For my father, Harry Puckett
1919–1997

Shadows Behind A Screen

by
Andrew Puckett

Dales Large Print Books
Long Preston, North Yorkshire,
England.

British Library Cataloguing in Publication Data.

Puckett, Andrew
    Shadows behind a screen.

    A catalogue record for this book is
    available from the British Library

    ISBN 1-85389-933-X pbk

First published in Great Britain by Constable & Company,
Ltd., 1998

Cover photography by arrangement with Last Resort Picture
Library

The right of Andrew Puckett to be identified as the author
of this work has been asserted by him in accordance with
the Copyright, Designs and Patents Act, 1988

Published in Large Print 1999 by arrangement with Constable
Publishers Ltd.

Dales Large Print is an imprint of
Library Magna Books Ltd.
Printed and bound in Great Britain by
T.J. International Ltd., Cornwall, PL28 8RW.

1

The cloudburst had smothered the light, turning morning into a sort of Twilight of the Gods, and the car-park outside the laboratory was full, so Harry had to manoeuvre the car round and look for a space in the main hospital park fifty yards away. In the rush to leave home, he'd forgotten his coat. He slammed the car door, locked it and started running, but was soaked through by the time he'd reached the locker room. He mopped his face with paper towels and tidied his hair as best he could before donning his white coat and running up the stairs.

'Morning, everyone.' He dumped his still dripping briefcase beside his desk. 'You'll notice I've left out the *good.*'

Graham Horfield, his deputy, smiled briefly. 'Joy's been looking for you, I'm afraid—'

Harry let out a groan.

'She said she wanted to see you as soon as you came in.'

Harry looked up at the clock on the wall. It was between a quarter and twenty past nine.

'It's almost as though she knew I was going to be late,' he said plaintively. 'Did she say what she wanted?'

Graham shook his head. 'No.'

Harry looked round, unwilling to go. 'Is everything all right here?'

'It's fine.'

'Well, better get it over with, I suppose.' He walked slowly over to the door, looked back. 'Pray for me,' he said, and left the room.

As he walked along the corridor, his shirt rubbed wetly against his neck and one of his socks squelched inside his shoe. His eyes were gritty from lack of sleep. It was, as Harry himself was to observe later, a totally lachrymose sort of day, the kind that could only get worse.

Joy's office was near the far end. *Apologise,* Harry told himself as he approached it, *don't antagonise her* ... The door was open and she looked up from her desk as Harry appeared.

'Good afternoon.'

'I'm sorry, Joy. Peter was ill again during the night and—'

'Close the door, please, and sit down.'

Harry did so. 'I called the doc—'

'I'm sorry to hear about Peter,' Joy continued evenly, her eyes hard on his face, 'but it is becoming a bit of a habit, isn't it?'

8

'I—'

'Not really the sort of example a department head should be setting his staff, is it?'

Harry found himself tunnelling his vision, concentrating on her mouth, the shapes her lips made as she framed each word. *God, she is so ugly,* he thought. *Ms Blobby made flesh* ... The thought cheered him a little and he said, 'I *am* sorry, Joy, but it was worse last night and I called the doctor first thing this morning.' Peter was his one-year-old son.

'What did the doctor say?'

'I don't know. I left home before he arrived.'

Joy's eyebrows lifted fractionally. 'You didn't wait for him?'

'No. I wish I had now,' he added deliberately.

'All right, that wasn't what I wanted to see you about.' She picked up an invoice from her desk and handed it to him. 'D'you know anything about this?'

Harry stared at it. 'Ah ...'

Joy waited. Harry said, 'Yes, it was me, I'm afraid.'

Her mouth tightened. 'How many times,' she said, 'have I asked you, *begged* you not to telephone orders? They must all go through me.'

'I know, Joy, and I'm sorry, but you

were off that day and it was urgent.'

'Then why didn't you at least tell me about it, leave me a message?'

'I forgot. I apologise.'

Joy wasn't mollified. 'What is this stuff, anyway? *Taq polynucleotide polymerase ...?*'

'It's a DNA primer, part of the project I'm working on with Dr Crowe.'

Far from soothing her, introduction of the Director's name seemed to inflame her all the more. 'And that gives you the right to telephone orders over my head, does it? And the price ...' A fleck of spittle flew from her mouth on to the desk. 'I don't suppose you bothered to check whether there's a cheaper alternative, did you?'

'There isn't—'

''Course, the budget's not your worry, is it? It's—'

'Why don't you go and speak to Dr Crowe about it?' Harry interrupted suddenly, his voice becoming thinner, flatter, as it always did when his control began to slip, more East London.

'Oh, I will,' she assured him. 'And I'm going to tell him—'

The phone rang and she snatched it up. 'Joy Manners ... Oh, really ... ? No, put it through.' She held out the receiver to him. 'A personal call for you—deal with it, please, then I'll finish what I have to say.'

'Harry Benedict speaking ... Oh, yes, doctor ...'

Joy watched a moment as the dark eyes in his thin, etched face stopped moving, then looked away. She wasn't listening, she was thinking: *What on earth did Tania see in him?*

Harry handed the phone back to her. 'That was my GP. He thinks Peter's got an ear abscess and is having him admitted to Children's Ward A.' He stood up. 'I'm going back to my lab now to tell my staff where I'll be, then, with your permission, I'm going over to see my son.' He stalked out, not bothering to wait for a reply. Joy watched him go, then, slowly, her lips pressed together and her eyes clamped shut.

Harry was wrong about Joy, she only seemed ugly when her face was bunched up—either with anger, as it had been, or with humiliation, as it was now.

Richard had been waiting to see Joy himself and, when he saw Harry's back retreating up the corridor, he went along to her room. Joy, sensing him, quickly recovered herself.

'Problems?' enquired Richard.

'You could say that.'

'Concerning himself?' Richard nodded in the direction of Harry's lab.

11

'What do you think?'

'Want to tell me about it?'

Joy hesitated. 'Shut the door.'

Richard did so. 'What happened?' he asked softly.

How different they are, she thought as she told him, and it was true—the fact of their both being department heads was almost all they had in common. Richard was shorter, at thirty-three a little older, and where Harry's face was naked, his own was hidden behind a reddish beard that some thought hid his persona as well. Like Joy, he spoke with a soft Dorset lilt.

'Needless to say,' Joy finished, 'the order was part of his precious project and he had the bloody gall to tell me to go and see the boss about it.'

'Why don't you do that?'

'Oh, don't you worry, I will—'

'Good, but Joy, why don't you cool down a bit first? Prepare a reasoned case, tell the boss that this sort of thing makes it impossible for you to work out the budget—you know how he's terrified of anything to do with that.'

Joy looked at him and nodded slowly. 'That's an idea ... yes, I'll do that.' She grimaced. 'But you know the worst of it—it turns out that Peter really is ill this time.'

Richard stiffened. 'Oh?'

12

'Yes, his GP rang while I was bawling him out. Seems he has an ear abscess and the doctor's having him admitted. Don't get me wrong. I'm sorry for the boy, but it's funny how Mr Bloody Benedict always manages to wriggle out from under.'

'Yes, it is, isn't it,' Richard agreed thoughtfully. 'Joy, I've just had another thought ...'

At that moment, 'Mr BB' was striding swiftly along the covered walkway that led to the Old Hospital. Rain-water spattered into the ground either side of him from the guttering and a fine spray drifted on the wind into his face ... Regis-on-Sea General consisted of this—the spider's web of buildings left by the Americans after the war, the long 'Nightingale' wards joined by passageways wide enough to take a jeep—and the New Hospital, a chunk of 'sympathetic nineties' architecture, which meant it was built of bricks rather than concrete and had recognisable roofs.

He pushed through the spring-loaded rubber doors, which flapped shut behind him, then started up the slight gradient towards Ward A. The floor was a dull nut brown, smoothed by more than five decades of feet and rubber tyres—an electric tug whirred past him now, towing a short line of trailers. The air was filled with the cabbagey-canteen smell common to all old hospitals. He turned a corner and crossed to the stainless-steel security doors of Children's A, incongruous against the aged concrete slabs, and pressed the intercom button above the combination lock.

'Children's Ward A, Student Nurse Ashfield speaking,' said a tinny, slightly adenoidal voice.

'I'm Harry Benedict—my son Peter's just been admitted, or he's about to be.'

There was a pause. 'I don't know anything about that. Could you hold on while I—'

'Would you get Sister Yate, please,' Harry cut in on her impatiently. 'Tell her it's Harry.'

'Sister's not here at the moment.'

Harry groaned in frustration, then a voice to his right said, 'You rang, sir?' and he looked up to see Sally Yate approaching him, holding a baby. Her face was dimpled with pleasure, as was the baby's.

'Sally ... Peter's ill and the doctor's arranged for him to be admitted ...'

Her smile vanished. She leaned across him and spoke tersely into the intercom. 'Nurse, it's Sister here—let us in, please.'

The lock clicked. Harry pushed open the door for her, then quickly followed.

'Ashfield said something about a sick

child coming as I was going to collect junior here from Ward B,' Sally said over her shoulder, 'but I had no idea it was Peter. What's the matter with him?'

'The doctor said an ear abscess, which might explain why he's been so restless the last couple of nights.'

'It might indeed,' she agreed.

They followed the corridor round to the left, passed Sally's office and then turned right into the duty room. The whole ward had been recently rebuilt, and the new duty room was a light, spacious area surrounded by separate cubicles, one for each sick child plus parent. As they approached the nurses' station, the young nurse there said, 'I've found it now,' and pointed at the list on the desk.

Sally regarded her coldly. 'Thank you, nurse. Perhaps you'd like to put Sebastian back in his cot—preferably without dropping him.'

The nurse swallowed, came round and took him. Sebastian began grizzling. Sally watched as she carried him to his cubicle, rolled her eyes at Harry in exasperation, then went to the nurses' station and ran her finger down the list. 'Yes, here we are, Benedict.' She looked up. 'Did your doctor call an ambulance, d'you know, Harry?'

'No, he said it would be quicker for Marie to bring him in.' Marie was Peter's

15

nanny. 'I'd have thought they'd have been here by now ...' He tailed off.

Sally leaned over, put her hand on his. 'It can't be that serious, or the doctor would've called an ambulance and waited with him.'

'Yeah, you're right.' He smiled, then gently disengaged his hand as Nurse Ashfield came back. He and Sally had been going out together for about a month.

The intercom buzzed and Sally answered it.

'Children's A, Sister speaking.'

'My name is Marie Davidson. I have Peter Benedict with me for admission. It's been arranged by ...'

Harry was already on his way back up the corridor as he recognised Marie's slightly husky voice. Sally said, 'Nurse, find Dr Miller and tell him we'll be using Number Three,' then followed him.

Harry reached the door, opened it and Marie came in, clutching Peter to her breast. He was wrapped in a blanket, his blond curls and thin, persistent cries his only tangible features. Hair and blanket were covered with tiny drops of moisture.

'Shall I take him, Marie?' Harry was saying.

'It's all right, thanks, I can manage.'

'This way, please,' Sally said crisply,

and led them back through the duty room to Cubicle Three, where Dr Miller, a young house officer with clean good looks, was already waiting with Nurse Ashfield. Sally explained why Peter had been brought in, then indicated Harry. 'This is his father—he works here in the microbiology lab.'

'Would you like to hold him while I examine him?' Dr Miller asked Harry.

'Let Marie do it,' Harry said. 'She was a nurse, she'll do it better than me.'

Marie sat down quickly on the chair. Peter still cried insistently. She eased him round so that he was facing forward, put one hand round him to hold his arms still, and the other round his forehead.

'That's great,' said Dr Miller. 'Just keep holding him like that.' He picked up the auroscope from the tray beside the chair and, holding the crown of Peter's head, inserted it into his ear and peered down it. Peter wriggled and squirmed and his screams rose to a crescendo. Sally watched Harry's face as his eyes clenched shut and his lips became a thin, bloodless line.

Dr Miller withdrew the auroscope. 'Just a few seconds more,' he said to Marie. He took a swab from its plastic tube and, inserting it into the ear, took up as much of the discharge as he could. He replaced it, scribbled on the tube, filled in a request form and handed them to Nurse Ashfield.

'Could you put "Urgent" stickers on these, please, Nurse, and get them into a container for the micro lab. I'll phone them myself in a minute.'

'Yes, Doctor,' she said, and was gone.

He turned to Sally. 'Get him into bed, get a paracetamol suppository into him ASAP and some Emla cream on to his arm for a drip. Please, sister,' he added with a smile, then turned to Harry. 'Mr—er—Benedict, a word with you, please.'

Sally said, 'I'll see you in my office, Harry.'

Harry gave her a nod, then looked down at Peter, who was still crying. He touched his head, then followed Miller out. The nurse was packaging the sample for the 'tube', the recently installed compressed air-system whereby material could be transported quickly round the hospital without the need for porters, much to their chagrin.

'Your GP was right to send him in,' Miller said. 'It's nothing to get too alarmed about, but it is nasty, so it's as well we've caught it at this stage.'

'It is an ear abscess, then?'

'Oh yes.'

'Staph?'

'I'd bet my month's salary on it. A paltry enough sum,' he added, and Harry smiled dutifully. 'Did he have a temperature last night?' Miller asked.

'Yes, he did. I gave him some Calpol, which seemed to calm him down, and then called Dr Ember this morning. I didn't dream it was this serious,' he added.

Miller touched his arm. 'Don't blame yourself. As I said, it's nothing to panic about. I've asked the lab for a preliminary Gram stain, so if it's what we think, I'll start him on Flucloxacillin as soon as the Emla cream's numbed his arm.'

'Good.'

'As I imagine you're already aware, Fluclox is the best antibiotic in the circumstances.' He smiled. 'I expect you know the figures better than I do—is it ninety-nine per cent of Staphs sensitive?'

'Ninety-eight per cent of wild strains, but only seventy to eighty per cent of hospital strains. Which this could well be,' Harry added gloomily.

'I've asked for a Direct Sensitivity to cover that possibility. It probably *will* be sensitive, though, so let's not anticipate problems, eh?' He paused. 'Will his mother be able to come in and stay with him?'

'She died six months ago,' Harry said tonelessly.

'I'm sorry—I didn't know.'

19

'There's no reason you should.' Mention of her somehow triggered Harry's memory and for an instant he could see Tania's face, hear her mocking voice ... *You're almost tall, dark and handsome, aren't you, Harry Benedict—but not quite ...*

'I'd better phone the lab,' Miller said after a pause and turned away.

Harry went back over to Peter's room, but when he looked through the glass door, Sally was administering the suppository while Marie tried to calm the child, and he didn't think he ought to interrupt. He felt suddenly at a complete loss, superfluous, then remembered Sally saying she'd see him in her office. He walked slowly back to it, a small room in the corridor just round from the duty room, and sat down to wait for her.

Her desk, while not exactly a mess, wasn't a model of tidiness either. He picked up a biro from where it had fallen on the floor and replaced it beside the winking computer terminal. He looked around.

Colourful charts adorned the walls, and also a newspaper cutting he hadn't noticed before. He stood up to look at it more closely. It showed Sally accepting an oversize cheque from the mayor, in recognition of the fund-raising she'd done for the ward. He smiled wryly, reflecting that the picture didn't do her justice. Yes, it showed how attractive she was, her curves, her chestnut curls and heart-shaped face, but Sally in the flesh was more than just attractive—she was beautiful.

There was a noise behind him and he turned to see her standing in the doorway, looking at him.

'I didn't realise you were so famous,' he said.

'Oh, that,' she said, looking pleased nevertheless. 'Well, he's a bit calmer now. Would you like to come and see him?'

'Sure.'

The phone rang. 'You go,' she said. 'Try not to disturb him too much.'

Peter was in a cot, still whimpering, but quietly now. Marie held his hand and sang softly to him. His blue eyes were fixed on her with total trust and the blond hair round his head glowed like a halo. Nurse Ashfield sat on the other side of the cot.

Thoughts tumbled through Harry's mind as he stood there watching them: *She's so much better with him than me, I'd never be able to do that ... is that a function of Marie, or of me ... or of Peter himself? God, he's so like Tania ...*

Time passed, then the door opened behind him and Sally beckoned him out.

'He's settled, then?' she said.

'Yeah.' He smiled. 'Marie's working her magic on him.'

'The lab have rung to say that the preliminary Gram stain's in the computer —I thought you'd like a look.'

Miller was studying the screen at the nurses' station. He looked up. 'Not really a surprise,' he said, and moved aside a little so that Harry could see.

Gram stain
Pus cells +++
Gram positive cocci in clumps +++

'I'll get him on a drip as soon as the Emla cream has worked. We should see an improvement by this evening.'

'Thanks, Doctor.' He turned to Sally. 'I'll just put my head in to Marie, then I'd better be getting back.'

'I'll come to the door with you,' she said.

She walked in silence beside him for a while, then said, 'He's going to be all right, Harry.'

He nodded. 'I know.'

They reached the door and she said, 'Speaking of this evening, I don't suppose you'll be wanting to go to the concert now, will you?' The Bournemouth Symphony Orchestra were playing at the Pavilion

22

that night and she'd persuaded him to take her.

Harry stopped. 'Lord, I'd forgotten about that.' He hadn't wanted to go anyway: classical music wasn't his scene and he'd been rather surprised it was hers, surprised too at the persistence with which she'd persuaded him. He'd put it down to middle-class education and values.

'D'you want me to stay with you?' she asked.

'No, you go—I know how you've been looking forward to it.'

'Shall I see if anybody here wants your ticket?'

'Oh, yeah—it'd be a shame to waste it.' He sighed. 'I'm sorry about this ...'

'It can't be helped.'

'I'll come over again at lunchtime—you'll tell me if there's any change before then, won't you?'

'Of course I will, Harry.' Impulsively, she pulled his head down and gave him a lingering kiss. 'Try not to worry. Mm?'

'Yeah. See you later.'

He opened the door and walked back down to the rubber flaps. Outside, it was still raining.

Bloody hell, he thought. *Why did this have to happen now? God, what a bloody mess ...*

2

The microbiology lab, although on the hospital site, was not actually Trust property; it was owned by the National Microbiology Service, and the 'border' between their respective territories was marked by a line of white stones. Harry passed through this (sometimes known as Checkpoint Crowe) into the entrance hall and up the stairs.

At the top he hesitated; he'd have liked to have looked at Peter's Gram stain himself, but the thought of having to ask Richard was more than he could stomach, so he turned left for his own department.

Graham looked up as he came in, and went over to him. 'How is he?' he asked in a low voice.

'Well, it's an ear abscess, like my GP thought. It looks like staph, so they've put him on Fluclox.'

'That ought to sort it. Is he comfortable?'

'He is now they've got some paracetamol into him. How're things here?' he said, changing the subject.

'OK. I think we've got another primary syphilis.' He showed Harry a pathology form. 'Referred to us from Celchester.'

Harry studied it, then looked up. 'Looks promising. Did they send a swab?'

'It's in the fridge with the others.'

'How many is that?'

'This makes six.'

Harry glanced up at the clock—today was Friday, he didn't want them hanging round over the weekend. 'If you set them up now, we've just about time for a PCR run.'

Graham hesitated. 'I know it's a bad time to ask, but I was hoping you'd let me have a half-day ...'

Harry didn't say anything and Graham continued in a low voice, 'The thing is, Carrie and I've got a problem we need to get sorted, and ...'

Harry nodded, touched his shoulder. 'You get everything set up, and I'll do the rest—OK?'

'Thanks, Harry,' Graham said, meaning it.

With an effort, Harry put his own problems to one side of his mind, went over to his desk and had started work on his weekly report when he became aware of a shadow hovering with intent a few feet away. He looked up.

'Yes, Karen?'

'I've done the work you set for me. The species of *Neisseria* ...'

'Oh, right. You'd better come and show me.'

Karen was a recent acquisition, a graduate with big brown eyes in a pretty, somehow innocent face that tantalised Harry's lust buds. He fetched her a chair.

'I gave you four cultures, didn't I? And you had to identify them using biochemical tests—right?'

'Yes, right.'

He smiled at her. 'So tell me.'

As she began speaking, he found himself wondering suddenly whether she was still a virgin ... *Shouldn't think so, not if she's been to university, and yet ...* He pushed the prurient thought away and tried to concentrate on what she was saying.

'So what in fact you've done,' he said when she'd finished, 'is to demonstrate the presence of DNA sequences. That's what all biological identification comes down to, recognition of DNA sequences ...' Other thoughts intruded now, which he also pushed away. 'These days, we tend to use more rapid methods ...'

'Isn't the PCR work you're doing on syphilis the same sort of thing?' she asked.

'That's right—the Polymerase Chain Reaction amplifies specific DNA and absolutely identifies *Treponema pallidum,* the organism that causes syphilis.'

'Why d'you do it on syphilis and not

other diseases?' she asked.

'Because *T. pallidum* can't be grown in the laboratory. So the next best thing is to demonstrate specific DNA in material taken from the primary lesion.'

She looked puzzled at this and he said, 'D'you not know the clinical stages of syphilis?'

'Not really, no.'

'Oh. Well, I'd better run through them for you.' He gathered his thoughts. 'Two weeks or so after sexual contact, the patient develops a genital lesion, rather like an ulcer—that's primary syphilis. A couple of weeks or so after that, it heals up and the patient thinks they've got nothing more to worry about.

'Well, they're wrong, because sooner or later, they develop secondary syphilis, which presents as a generalised body rash. Large Pox, it used to be called in Shakespeare's time, to differentiate it from Smallpox. It's what he meant when he said someone was poxed.'

'I knew that, but I didn't know *why* before.'

'It was a much more common disease in those days.' He grinned at her as he warmed to his subject. 'So common, in fact, that the Roman Catholic Church decided they had to appoint a patron saint for syphilitics. After much soul searching, their choice fell on St Dennis.'

She laughed out loud.

'Oh, I kid you not. Certainly makes you wonder about their morals in those days. Penitent sufferers used to pray to St Dennis to cure them, and sometimes their prayers were answered, because the rash would go away and not come back.'

'But not always?'

'No. In other cases, the disease became latent, perhaps for as long as ten years or more before the final, tertiary stage. That's the one that destroys your nervous system and makes you go blind. It's also incurable and causes megalomania.'

'Oh yes, didn't Hitler have it?'

'He very likely did. Al Capone certainly did, and Henry VIII's another probable, so one way and another, *T. pallidum*'s got a lot to answer for. Which is why, coming back to PCR, it's so important to be able to identify the primary stage. Look, I'll show you ...'

He jumped up and went over to Graham. 'Can I borrow that path form a minute? Thanks.'

Graham winked at the others in the lab as if to say, *He's off again* ...

'Here we have a female,' Harry said, 'who presents at clinic with a genital lesion. She'd had sexual contact three weeks earlier and the clinician suspects

28

early primary syphilis—but he's not sure, because the lesion is difficult to examine in a female. It could be herpes virus, for instance. So he takes some blood and sends it to us ...' Enthusiasm lit his mobile face and animated his wiry body as he developed his theme and she thought, *He's dishy—I see now how he got his reputation ...*

'All we can do at the moment,' he continued, 'is to test it for antibodies to *T. pallidum,* which haven't had time to fully develop yet, which is why we get these inconclusive results. All they do is tell the clinician he *might* be right, but then again, he might not.'

'What about the patient all this time?'

'Oh, she'll be treated for syphilis, but the clinician needs to know, for legal reasons, and also for contact tracing—which is why we're trying to develop a PCR that will actually pinpoint the specific DNA of *T. pallidum.*'

'Does it work?'

Harry sighed. 'That's the billion buck question. It *seems* to, sometimes, but there's a hell of a long way to go. Which DNA sequence should we choose? Should we use more than one? What primers should we use? How should we prepare the sample? It's endless.'

'It's fascinating,' she said, looking at him.

'It's also frustrating and thankless. But yes, it is fascinating.' He glanced up at the clock. 'I didn't mean to go off at such a tangent ... Where were we? Oh yes, *Neisseria*. You've done the biochemical tests, now try some serological ones. Carl ...'

He called another of his staff over and asked him to oversee Karen's work, then turned, without much enthusiasm, back to his report.

He'd just got into it again when the door opened and a figure came quietly in.

Oh no, he thought. It was Amina Khatoon, who worked in Richard's lab. She came over to his desk.

'Hi, Amina.'

'Can I have a word, please, Harry?'

'Sure.' He waved at the chair Karen had just vacated.

She sat. 'I'm sorry about Peter.'

'Thanks.' He paused. 'News travels fast.'

'It was me who did the preliminary Gram stain.'

'Oh ... well, thanks for being so quick about it.'

'That's all right. Are they treating him?'

Harry briefly told her what they were doing, then said, 'Anyway, how can I help you?'

'It's difficult.' Her tongue touched her

lips. 'I don't want to be a nuisance, but ...'

Strange, he thought, *how her voice still has that slight singsong quality, even though she was born over here ...* She was slender and dusky, with drapes of dark hair that framed her graceful features.

'I don't want to be a nuisance,' she repeated, 'but I'd like to ask you a favour.'

'Ask away.'

'My tutor, at the university, says that we should be sorting out now what we are going to do for our dissertations. For my Master's degree.'

'Oh, yes.'

'Well, I happened to mention to him that you were working with PCR and he said that if at all possible I should do my dissertation on that ...'

'Ah ...'

Her tongue touched her lips again. 'I wondered whether it would be possible for me to be involved, to help in some way ...'

She tailed off.

I owe her, he thought, *but not this.* 'It might be difficult, Amina. You see, we've only just started the preliminary work—we're still trying to iron out all the problems at the moment.'

'Is there no way I could help? As a pair of hands?'

31

He hesitated. 'Let me think about it, and I'll come back to you. OK?'

'OK, Harry,' she said, knowing he wouldn't. 'Thanks.'

She got up and left the room, as quietly as she'd come in. Harry watched her go, then turned once again to his report. But he couldn't concentrate ... *If I can get this project to work—Crowe'll claim most of the credit, of course, but maybe I can use it as the basis for a PhD ... Why does Amina make me feel so guilty ... ?*

The phone on his desk rang and he picked it up.

'Genito-urinary lab.'

'It's Dr Crowe, Harry,' said the familiar fruity voice. 'Could you spare me a few minutes?'

'Of course, Doctor. I'm on my way.'

Dr Crowe's office was in the middle of the building, near the top of the stairs. Harry tapped on the open door.

'Come in, Harry. Have a seat.' Crowe indicated the armchair that was positioned sideways in front of his desk.

Harry sank into it, reflecting that Crowe must have attended a psychology course at some stage, since the chair's height, or lack of it, meant that he had to gaze up, sideways, at Crowe's face across the expanse of his desktop.

'I'm sorry to hear about your son,

Harry. You've been over to see him, I understand?'

'Yes ...' *He's in his kindly old uncle mode,* Harry thought as he told him what had happened, and it was true; with his honest, open face filled with concern, his fluffy semicircle of white hair and spotted bow tie, Dr Theodore Crowe, Director of Regis National Microbiology Laboratory, did look rather like every child's favourite uncle.

'Well, they seem to be doing all the right things,' he said when Harry had finished. 'I've no doubt you'll see an improvement before the end of the day.'

'I hope so.'

'I'm sure you will.' Crowe paused, then his voice dropped a semi-quaver as he switched mode. 'I've had a somewhat aggrieved Joy in here complaining that you've been ordering expensive materials without going through her.'

'Ah, yes. It was my fault, I'm afraid, Dr Crowe.' He knew from Crowe's tone that he had to admit at least some guilt. 'It was the day she was away last week and we needed the new primers urgently for the PCR run.'

'Well, I can sympathise with that, obviously, but Joy is worried about the budget implications, as, indeed, she has every right to be. She feels there may have been a cheaper alternative.'

'There isn't, Doctor,' said Harry, shaking his head. 'If you remember, we thought this particular primer might improve the specificity. There isn't another source for it. It was just unfortunate I forgot to tell her about it the next day.'

'Yes, it was rather.' Crowe paused to allow this to sink in. 'Couldn't you have waited until she returned so that she could have done the ordering?'

'I could have, yes, but it would have put us back several days.'

'Several *days?*'

Harry hesitated. 'Dr Crowe, Joy never orders anything urgently—it's always by second-class post. I didn't think we had the time to spare.'

Crowe considered him for a moment, then said, 'Well, Joy has put a suggestion to me herself that might solve the problem, and I'm minded to go along with it.'

Harry tensed.

'She says that if she were to play an active part in the project, then she'd be able to appreciate its needs better and do any urgent ordering herself.'

Oh my God ... Harry fought for self-control.

He took a breath and said steadily. 'Well, I can see how you think it might solve one problem, but isn't there a risk it might create other, worse problems?'

'In what way?'

Joy's chin on my shoulder, pokin' her nose into every orifice ... 'Well, as laboratory manager, Joy does already have an awful lot on her plate, I can't see how she'd be able to spare the time ... Also, to be perfectly honest, Doctor, I think she might have difficulty understanding the scientific principles involved.'

Crowe chuckled. 'You may have a point there.' Harry held his breath. 'But I still feel she'll be less of a problem if we take her on board with us.'

'But—'

'With your eloquence, Harry, I'm sure you'll be able to help her understand—it only requires a little good will on both sides.'

Harry didn't speak. He was speechless.

'Well, now,' continued Crowe, 'having got that out of the way, how's the project going?'

Oh, ecstasy ... with one quantum leap, you make life impossible, then demand a fuckin' progress report. Harry swallowed. 'Well, we have had better results with the new primer I ordered ...' *Better not push it.* 'We've just set up another run with six possible primaries. I'll be staying late tonight anyway, because of Peter, so I'll run the electrophoresis tests then.'

'Have you changed any of the other criteria? If you remember, we were discussing the preparation of the specimens.'

'No, I haven't—Graham and I can only manage one change at a time on our own ...' *Oh, no ...*

'Well, then, there's something Joy can help you with—she did say how keen she was to get involved in some practical work.'

Over my dead body. 'Can I think about that, Dr Crowe?'

Crowe leaned back and exhaled, his habitual 'end of discussion' signal. 'By all means, Harry. But do try to involve her in some way, won't you? I'm sure you'll find it's for the best.'

Harry got to his feet. 'I'll—I'll show you the results of this run on Monday, shall I, Dr Crowe?'

'Please, Harry.'

As he left the room, Crowe stared after him and allowed a small smile to play over his lips.

Silently, impotently, Harry gibbered with fury. *How the bloody hell did she manage it ... to think it up ... persuade Crowe ...?*

Then he caught sight of Richard coming up the stairs. For a microsecond, they stared at each other, read each other's minds ... and Harry recognised beyond all doubt the instigator of this new crown of thorns.

You bastard, he thought as he stalked back to his lab. *You just can't stop, can you?*

3

The rain had stopped by the time Harry walked back over to the Old Hospital at lunchtime to see Peter. Sag-bellied clouds still drove low across the September sky, but the air was clearer now, lighter, and his spirits lifted with it. He'd phoned the ward during the morning to be told that Peter was about the same.

Sally released the security lock from the nurses' station and he went through to the duty room.

'How is he?'

Sally hesitated. 'There's still no change, although we wouldn't necessarily have expected it at this stage. His temperature's still a bit high ... He was sleeping when I last looked in.'

'Is Marie still with him?'

'Yes.' She gave a wry smile. 'I don't think the proverbial wild horses would drag her away. Why don't you go in?'

He went over and eased the door open. Marie looked round from where she was sitting beside Peter. He raised a hand in greeting and she smiled wanly back. A drip hung from a hook and ran into Peter's arm.

Harry sat down, put his hand on Peter's forehead. It was hot and damp. Peter moaned slightly, his eyes opened, then closed again without really focusing.

'The sister says we shouldn't expect any improvement yet,' she whispered.

'I know. It's horrible though, seeing him like this.'

'Yes.'

Peter moaned again, stirred, and she took his hand, stroked it. 'It's all right, Peter, I'm here, and so's Daddy ...' His eyelids flickered, but her voice seemed to calm him and he settled back into an uneasy sleep.

She turned anxiously to Harry. 'We should see some improvement before long, shouldn't we?'

'Yes.' He watched Peter's face for a moment, then closed his eyes as emotions chased each other through his head.

When he felt calmer, he said, 'Antibiotics always take a while to work, but I'm sure we'll see something by this evening.'

'Oh, I hope so.'

'We will.' They sat in silence for

a while. *She looks older,* he thought inconsequentially. The lines in her face seemed more noticeable, as did the streaks of grey in her hair. He said, 'Marie, have you had any lunch yet?'

'Mm? Oh yes, I had a sandwich a little while ago.'

'D'you mind if I get some quickly while I can?'

'Of course not. I'll be here.'

'Thanks, Marie—for everything. I won't be long.'

Sally was still at the nurses' station, her fingers skimming over the keyboard as she cross-checked information on the computer. She looked up as he approached.

He said, 'Y'know, it's a funny thing ... for nearly ten years now I've been reading comments on path forms about patients with infections and temperatures, but this is the first time I've actually *seen* it.'

She smiled at him. 'Well, it's not the first time I've seen it. You worry too much.'

'Yeah, I suppose so.' He looked up. 'Did you find anyone who wanted the ticket?'

'Yes, Nick Miller's coming with me.'

'Good, I'm glad you'll have company.' He took a breath. 'I think I'll go and get a bite of lunch while I can.'

'I'd come with you, only Jane's not back yet and I don't know where Nurse

Ashfield's got to.' Jane Radford was the staff nurse. 'Besides, I'm on standby for Ward B.'

'Oh, that's ridiculous!' Harry said. Ward B was for older children and was a little way down the main corridor.

'It is, isn't it, but the sister's off sick and there it is. You go on.'

'All right. See you later.'

The canteen was surprisingly full. Harry found a tray and chose shepherd's pie as being the most easily digestible meal there, then looked around amid the chatter and clink of cutlery for somewhere to sit.

Amina was sitting by herself at an empty table. She hadn't seen him. As he looked round for somewhere else to sit, Richard came in and joined the lunch queue. Their eyes met—briefly, hostilely. *Sod you,* Harry thought, and made his way over to Amina.

'Mind if I join you?'

She looked up, startled. 'Er—no. Of course not.' She was wearing a brightly coloured dress which set off her skin tones and the gloss of her hair without being self-consciously ethnic.

'Thanks.' He sat down.

She looked at her plate, not knowing what to say. Harry took a forkful of shepherd's pie.

She said, 'Is Peter any better?'

40

'Not really, no. The antibiotic needs time to work.'

'I'm sure it will.'

'Yeah.' He took another mouthful of pie. 'How've you been keeping?'

'Oh, pretty good. You know how it is.'

'I don't, actually.'

'Well, it's ...' She smiled and shrugged. 'It's OK.'

'Working hard for your Master's, are you? Staying in every night?'

'Most nights, yes.'

'You know the saying about all work and no play ...?'

'It's important to me, this degree.'

'You still need some pleasures in life.'

She's blushing, he thought, watching her face as the blood percolated the pigments of her skin. *Why am I doing this to her?* A medley of answers rushed through his head and Richard sat down a couple of tables away.

'When's your final exam?' he asked her. 'Next summer, isn't it?'

'That's right.'

'Well, you shouldn't have any problems, not a swot like you.' He ate some more pie.

'That's easy for you to say. And as I told you this morning, there is still the dissertation ...'

As she spoke, an idea formed in his mind

41

and he said slowly, 'I've been thinking about that and it's possible we might be able to help each other.'

'You mean with the PCR work? Oh Harry, that would be wonderful!'

Exposed to her huge eyes, it was as though he was seeing her naked again and he felt his glands glow as he remembered how soft her body was, how it trembled ...

He tried to push the thoughts away. 'D'you understand the principles behind PCR?' he asked.

'I understand them in theory. You use primers and nucleotides to select and amplify a specific sequence of DNA, is that right?'

'Pretty much. It's—'

'My tutor said that instead of looking for a needle in a haystack, it was like turning the needle *into* a haystack.'

Harry laughed. 'That's pretty good, that's exactly what it's like—when it works.'

She laughed with him, then said, 'But it doesn't always work, you were telling me?'

'No, it does not.'

'What's the problem, d'you think?'

He took a breath and began explaining what he was trying to do, the problems he was having and how he needed to compare the various methods of preparation. She listened carefully, taking it all in, making observations and suggestions.

'And you think I could help you with that, and get enough material for my dissertation?' she said when he'd finished.

'I think it's possible, yes.' *And having you working with me might help keep Joy out of it ...*

'That would be marvellous. You've no idea how I've been searching for a—'

'For a needle in a haystack?'

They both started laughing again.

'Mind if I join in the fun?' Sally put her tray beside Harry's and sat down.

Oh, bloody hell. 'Er, Sally, this is Amina Khatoon. She works with me in the lab.'

'Hi.' Sally smiled brightly at her, appraising her.

'Amina, this is Sally Yate, she's the —er—ward sister in the ward where Peter is. Is there any change?' he asked Sally.

'Not in the short time since you left me, no.'

'Marie's still with him?'

'Of course she is.' She leaned over and squeezed his hand, spoke close to his ear. 'I told you, Harry, you worry too much. He's doing fine.' Her face and body language bespoke their relationship as clearly as if they'd both been nude. She straightened up, looked over at Amina, then back at

43

Harry. 'Anyway, are you going to share the joke with me?'

'We were just talking shop,' Harry said.

'Shop? Then laboratory life must be more fun than you've led me to believe. Perhaps I should try it.'

Amina said, 'Excuse me, I must be going.' She stood, took her tray over to the stacker, walked quickly away.

'Have I said something wrong?' demanded Sally, watching her as she walked out of the canteen.

'Harry—' she turned back to him— 'have you been having an affair with her or something?'

'No,' he said.

Richard quickly stacked his own tray and followed Amina out. He caught up with her by the lab car-park.

'Amina, are you all right?'

'Leave me alone.'

'Is that what you really want?'

'Yes! It's what I said, isn't it?'

He hesitated. 'All right ... if it *is* really what you want.'

'No ... don't go, please, Richard.' She caught his arm. 'I'm so *stupid* ...'

'Come over to my car.' He put his arm around her shoulders and led her over to his ancient Triumph Spitfire.

'It's not exactly luxurious, but at least it's

44

private,' he said, unlocking the passenger door. 'In you get.' He shut the door and let himself in the other side.

'I'm so stupid ...' she said again.

'Aren't we all, sometimes?'

'Setting myself up like that ...' She turned her eyes to him. 'I have tried to keep away from him, but I thought I was all right now ... so I asked him this morning about my dissertation.'

'I did warn you not to.'

'He said it would be difficult, and I accepted that, but then he came and sat with me in the canteen.'

'I know. I saw.'

'He said I could help him with his project after all. He was being so nice and I thought—I really thought ... then *she* came in. I—I hadn't realised he ...' With a choking noise, she began to cry, quietly at first, then with fierce, intense sobs. Richard put his arm round her as best he could over the transmission tunnel and stroked her head.

'That's right,' he said, feeling totally inadequate, 'have a good cry.'

After a little, the gusts subsided and she lay loosely in his arms, her cheek against his tweed jacket.

'Why am I like this, Richard?' she said tonelessly. 'Why can't I accept?'

'I don't know, Amina. Because you're the

45

person you are, I suppose.' He hesitated, then said slowly, 'I do think you should consider getting out. Leaving, getting away from here altogether.'

She sat up and found her handkerchief, blew into it. 'I *have* thought about it, but ... well, jobs aren't that easy to find and, besides, there's my Master's degree—I can't imagine another place would let me go on doing that.'

'Some would. I know Joy would give you a good reference and I'm sure Dr Crowe would as well.'

'Then there's my house. I have negative equity, you know.' She grimaced. 'I'm very British.'

'Couldn't you go back to your parents, just for a while?'

'No, Richard. When a Muslim tells his daughter she's no longer his daughter, he means it.'

He thought for a second. 'Why don't you go and talk to your building society? There must be some way you could buy another house on the same terms as you have now.'

'All right, I'll talk to them.' She paused. 'You seem very determined to get rid of me.'

'Don't be daft—it's just that I don't think you can go on like this.'

'You're right, I can't. I must grow up

and stop being a silly girl. Pull myself together.'

'That's not what I meant.'

'No, but it's what *I* mean ... I *must* ...'

'Amina, look at me.' He held her shoulders. 'You say you can't go on like this, and yet I have the feeling that all the things you've said to me are excuses for doing just that. Are you sure you've told me everything?'

Her face was perfectly still for a moment, like dark marble, then it crumpled again.

'Let it come out,' he said, holding her. 'Don't hold anything back ...'

Later, after she'd finished, she detached herself and tried to smile. 'And d'you know something, Richard, even my bike's got a puncture, so I had to walk in this morning.'

'Not your day,' he said quietly, his eyes glittering dangerously. Then: 'D'you want a lift home tonight?'

'That would be nice, Richard, thank you. Shall we go back now?'

'Are you sure?'

'Yes.' She nodded vigorously. 'Yes.'

As they approached the lab entrance, Harry came round the corner from the hospital.

'You go on up, Amina,' Richard said. 'I'll be along.'

She gave him a scared look, then hurried

inside and up the stairs.

'I want a word with you,' Richard said.

Harry stopped and looked at him. 'I didn't mean to upset her like that,' he said quietly. 'And I'm sorry—'

'I don't believe you. I saw you go over to her, quite deliberately, after you saw me come in—'

'That's true, but I didn't realise she still felt so strongly about me, and I didn't think Sally was coming in. I was trying to help her with her dissertation.'

'Like hell! You were teasing her to get at me.'

'No, I was—'

'I don't believe you.'

Harry took a breath. 'Well, I'm afraid that has to be your problem.'

'If I see you talking to Amina again,' Richard said with deathly intensity, 'I swear I'll make you regret it.'

'You?' Harry said incredulously. He was the fitter and stronger and they both knew it.

'Yes, me,' Richard said, taking a pace towards him.

With a ping, a filament inside Harry's head snapped. 'Y'know what your problem is, don't you?' he said conversationally. 'You fancy reamin' it yourself, don't you, only she ain't 'aving any, 'cos—'

Richard swung at him, but Harry was

ready for it; he swayed easily out of the way, then jabbed Richard hard in the solar plexus.

Joy burst out from the lobby.

'Stop that, *now!*'

4

Richard doubled over, retching and holding his belly.

'Up to my office, now,' Joy snapped at them.

Harry looked for a moment as though he was going to argue, then went inside and started up the stairs. Richard pulled himself upright with an effort and followed him.

'Sit down,' she said when they reached her office.

They sat. Richard was still deathly pale. Joy stared down at them in silence.

'I didn't start this—' Harry began.

'Be quiet!' Joy regarded them a few more moments before speaking.

'I still can't believe this. Department heads ... the most senior members of staff here after me, and I find you *brawling*, in full view of anyone who might be passing ...' She took a breath, looking from one to the other of them.

'I don't want to hear any excuses. I'm taking official disciplinary action against both of you, in writing. In it, I will state that if anything like this ever occurs again, you will be instantly dismissed. Is that clear?'

'I protest that I didn't start this,' Harry said thickly.

'I saw what happened,' Joy said softly to him. 'I also heard. Get out. Not you,' she said as Richard stood up as well. 'I haven't finished with you yet.'

After the door had closed behind Harry, Joy sat down at her desk and said tiredly, 'What the bloody hell are you playing at, Richard?'

Richard swallowed. 'You didn't see what he did to Amina.'

'I said I didn't want any excuses.' After a pause, she said, 'Well, what did he do to Amina?'

Richard told her what he'd seen in the canteen and some of what Amina had told him.

Joy said, 'That doesn't make any difference—what I said stands.'

'But—'

'Listen.' She stared him down. 'He was right, you *did* start it. I should have come down harder on you than him.'

'I know that, Joy, and I apologise,' Richard said. 'But you must listen as well.'

'Don't you *dare* tell me to—'

'No, Joy. Listen ...' Richard got up and approached her desk. 'This was a happy place once, d'you remember those days, three years ago, before *he* came here?'

'I don't need reminding.'

'He started undermining you from the moment he arrived and he's *still doing it.* He seduced—I know it's an old-fashioned idea, but it's true—he *seduced* Amina, and when her father found out, he cut her off, cast her out ...'

'But then he got tired of her and decided he fancied Tania, *my fiancée,* instead.'

'This isn't helping, Richard.'

'And Tania was misguided enough to go and live with him, and then, when she realised her mistake, he killed her—'

'Richard, stop it,' Joy said sharply. 'It was an *accident,* you saw the state he was in afterwards.'

'Didn't take him long to get over it, though, did it? And then take up with Amina again as a bit of home comfort.'

'It takes two, Richard.'

'Then he decides he fancies that slag on the Children's Ward, so poor old Amina gets the chop again. And today, I find him teasing her, leading her on, then flaunting Sister Slag in front of her.' Flecks of spittle were flying from his mouth now. 'She can't leave 'cos she can't sell her house, she can't

51

even go back to her family. she's trapped here with him ... this place is never going to be happy again until he's *gone.*'

'And now, thanks to you,' Joy said coldly, 'the job of getting rid of him is going to be that much harder.'

Richard sank back on to his chair.

'I'm sorry, Joy,' he whispered.

'So am I.'

'What are we going to do?'

'I've no idea. But you are right about one thing—he's got to go ...'

Harry did something he very rarely did at work—he went to his car where he found a pack of cigarettes and smoked two of them. After that, he went back to his lab, checked that everyone knew what they were doing, then sat at his desk and forced himself to do some more work on his report.

Richard went out too, but only to breathe in some of the cool, fresh air, allow his pulse rate to subside and the ache in his belly to fade a little. Then he returned to his department. Amina got up and went over to him.

'Are you all right?' she asked in a low, anxious voice. 'What happened?'

He forced a smile. 'I'm fine and I'll tell you later.' He went to his desk, but not to work. He sat and brooded.

At twenty past five, Harry went back over to Ward A. Nurse Ashfield let him in and he walked through to the duty room. Sally was at the nurses' station, looking down at something while Dr Miller leaned over her, pointing, his arm half round her.

Doctors and nurses, Harry thought, *how sweet* ... and, as though by telepathy, they looked up.

'Ah, Mr Benedict,' Miller said, straightening. 'We've been trying to get hold of you.'

'Why?' Harry went over to them. 'Is he worse?'

'I'm afraid he is, a little. He doesn't seem to be responding to the antibiotic and I've just this minute asked the micro lab to read the Direct Sensitivity early. They weren't very keen, I might add.'

'They wouldn't be,' said Harry, 'not after only seven hours. Can I see him?'

The phone rang and Sally snatched it up. 'Children's A, Sister Yate ... What, *now?* Oh, all right.' She put the phone down, shaking her head. 'I don't believe it, they need me in Ward B to put in an IV drug. I'm sorry, I'll have to go. Jane's in Number Six if you need anything.' She hurried out.

'Can I see my son now?' Harry asked Miller again.

'Sure—just go in. Your nanny's with him.'

Harry walked over, gently opened the door and let himself in. Marie looked round, her face drawn and white. In contrast, Peter's was red and puffy, swollen down one side. A damp flannel lay across his forehead. Harry leaned over and touched his cheek with the back of his hand—it was burning hot. Peter stirred, moaned, began grizzling.

Marie said, 'It's all right, Peter, I'm here,' and wiped his face gently with a fresh flannel. She stroked his hand and after a little, his cries subsided.

Harry let himself down on the other chair. 'How long's he been like this?'

'Not very long.' Marie swallowed. 'It came on so suddenly. Are they *doing* anything out there?'

'They've asked the lab to try and read the Direct Sensitivity test early. They'll probably change the drug.' He let out a sigh. 'Of all the luck, a resistant strain …'

'Shh. It'll be all right, I'm sure it will.'

'Sorry.' He grimaced. 'Save your comfort for him, Marie.'

She gave him a pallid smile, touched his shoulder, then returned to stroking Peter's hand.

A couple of minutes later, Peter started

crying again. Harry stood up abruptly and said, 'I can't stand any more of this, I'm going to find out what's going on.'

As he came into the duty room, Nurse Ashfield was walking away from the station.

'Nurse—have you heard from the lab yet?' he called out to her.

'That's them now.' She pointed to the receiver, lying on the desk. 'I'm—'

'Well, thank Christ for that!'

She glared angrily at him. 'I'm just going to find Sister—'

'Oh, for God's sake, can't the staff nurse take it?'

'No,' she snapped back at him. 'You ought to know about that.'

'Where's Dr Miller?'

'*I* don't know ...' She hurried away before he could say any more, leaving him staring after her.

Richard was studying the plate under the lamp with a hand lens when Joy came in and went over to him.

'I thought you were coming to see me.'

Richard glanced up. 'I was—I've got to read this first. Urgent Direct Sensitivity. I'll be along.'

Joy picked up the form. 'It's Peter Benedict ...'

'Yeah, and the organism's resistant to Fluclox.'

'Poor little bugger—sorry, Amina!' She smiled sheepishly over to where Amina was waiting, then glanced at the plate. 'Is it readable?'

'Just about.' Richard looked round at her in irritation. 'I'll be along, Joy—all right?' It was a measure of their relationship that he could talk to her like this, even after the afternoon's events.

She held up her hands in mock surrender. 'OK, OK, I'm going.'

Amina could feel the humiliation, the misery rising inside her anew like a malignant tide. She tried to swallow it down, failed ...

'Richard,' she said, 'I'll wait for you downstairs, all right?'

'Mm? Oh, OK, Amina.'

He studied the plate a few moments more, then quickly pencilled the results on to the path form—S for sensitive, R for resistant, next to the name of each antibiotic. Then he called up the Patient Systems Program on the computer, found Peter's file and keyed the results in.

As Joy came out of Richard's lab, she saw Dr Crowe turn into his room and shut the door. She went to her own room and sat down. She wondered for a moment about going to speak to him, then changed her mind.

Richard phoned the ward.

'Children's Ward A, Student Nurse Ashfield.'

'Microbiology lab here—can I speak to Sister, please?'

'Er ... I'm afraid she's not here at the moment. Can I get Staff Nurse for—?'

'You ought to know the regulations by now, nurse—it has to be Sister. Will you get her please, *now?* This is urgent.'

'The lab results are in the computer, but the nurse has had to go and find Sister,' Harry told Marie.

'*Why*, for goodness' sake?'

'The lab won't give urgent results over the phone any more—there were too many mistakes being made on the wards. Now, we put them into the computer, then tell the ward sister when they're in.'

'But that's absolutely ridiculous! Surely, in the circumstances they could—?'

'Sister's in Children's Ward B, I'm sure she won't be long.'

Sally came into the duty room, saw the phone lying on the desk and picked it up 'Hello ...'

'Is that Sister?'

'Yes—Sister Yate, Children's Ward A speaking.'

'At last!' Richard said. 'The Direct Sensitivity results for Peter Benedict are in the computer.'

'Oh, good. Thank you.'

'Sister, d'you realise how long I've been waiting here, surely you could have—?'

'Well, don't blame *me* for that!' Sally snapped, and slammed the phone down. She looked up to see Nurse Ashfield hurrying in. 'Nurse—where have you *been?*'

'I—looking for you, sister.'

'I was in Ward B—you knew that.'

'I know—we must have missed each other.'

'Oh, never mind. D'you know where Dr Miller is?'

'I—no. Shall I go and—?'

'No, *don't* go and look for him. I'll bleep him.'

Richard slowly replaced his own receiver, then shook himself out of his reverie and went along to Joy's office. Joy wasn't there.

'Perhaps just as well,' he muttered to himself. He went downstairs, changed out of his lab coat and went to look for Amina.

She was in the tea room, staring out of the window.

'Are you ready?' he asked her.

She turned. 'Oh, yes. You've just missed Joy. She said she'd see you on Monday.'

'Oh, right.'

Richard pulled the main door shut and they walked in silence to his car, each shrouded in their own thoughts. It wasn't until Richard was driving away that he said, 'Are you feeling any better now?'

She was looking straight ahead, through the windscreen.

'Yes,' she said. 'Thank you.'

Sally bleeped Dr Miller, then called up the Patient Systems Program and she and Nurse Ashfield looked at Peter's results. As Miller came in, she said, 'Here's why he isn't improving.'

He studied the screen. 'Resistant to Flucloxacillin—so Mr Benedict was right. He said it might be a hospital strain,' he added in reply to Sally's enquiring look. He turned back to the screen. 'What have we got here ... ah! It's sensitive to Gentamicin—we'll get him on that straight away.'

At 6.15, Harry told Marie to go home.

'I don't like to leave him,' she said. 'I feel as though I'm deserting him.'

'Marie, he's going to be all right now. He's looking better already.'

59

This was true—although the Gentamicin hadn't had time to work yet, Peter had been given something to reduce his temperature and was now sleeping more peacefully.

'You've been a saint today,' Harry continued, 'but you've got your own life. Trevor'll be back home by now, won't he?'

'Yes ... Well, if you're sure ...'

'I am sure.'

'You'll let me know how he is?'

'Of course I will.'

Sally had gone off duty at six, but her replacement, Clare Roberts, assured Harry that she would keep a special eye on Peter, so he went back to the lab to read the final stages of the PCRs as he'd promised Dr Crowe. Also, as he admitted to himself, to try and take his mind off things.

By eight o'clock, Peter was no better, but since he'd only started the Gentamicin two hours earlier, no one realised how bad things were until nine, when his condition abruptly deteriorated. Dr Whitaker, the senior registrar on duty, phoned Dr Crowe at home. Harry stood beside her, fidgeting.

'I've got two other antibiotics available,' she said, looking at the computer screen, 'Clindamycin and Vancomycin. Should I start him on one of those?'

'No—the Gentamicin must be given more time to work,' Crowe told her.

'Phone me in an hour if he's no better.'

An hour later, he was worse. He was transferred to Intensive Care where he was given the other antibiotics, sedated, paralysed and put on a ventilator. Harry sat beside him, totally impotent now as the monitors clicked and bleeped around him.

As a last, desperate measure, Peter was given Dopamine, to improve renal function and ward off heart failure, but it was all too late—the bacteria had broken out from the site of infection and were now circulating freely in his bloodstream, causing all his organs to fail. At a little after midnight, Peter Benedict drew a final, fluttering breath and died of an overwhelming staphylococcal septicaemia.

Harry was frozen. For the last two hours, he'd been with him, his face growing more wax-like as Peter's life slipped away.

'I can't tell you how desperately sorry I am,' Dr Whitaker said to him. 'Is there anyone you can stay with, anyone who could come and collect you?'

Harry shook his head. 'No.' It came out as a croak.

'Who's your GP?'

'Er ... Dr Ember.'

'I'll phone him.'

'No. Please—don't phone anyone. I just want to be left alone.'

'Go and see Dr Ember tomorrow morning—will you promise me you'll do that? He will be able to help you.'

'Yes.'

'I'm going to give you some sedative tablets for tonight. They won't stop you grieving, but they will give you some sleep, which you're going to need. And I'll phone for a taxi to take you home.'

Again Harry shook his head. 'No, please, I'll be all right.'

'Mr Benedict, you're in shock. I don't think you're in a fit state to drive.'

He spoke slowly. 'I'm not in a fit state to talk to a taxi driver either. Please ... I don't have far to go and I won't be a danger to anyone. I just want to go home and be on my own. Please ...'

She studied him. 'All right,' she said at last. 'I'll get you those tablets now—but don't take them until you *are* home.'

Harry walked to his car on legs that functioned, feet whose steps he could hear, and yet they—no, *he*—was quite different, somewhere else. The night was crystal quiet, the stars infinite. As he put the key into the car door he thought, *The last time I did this was this morning ...*

The engine sounded strange and faraway, but it was him. The drumming of the tyres on the road, the car door slamming when he got home, the latch on his front door snapping to—familiar sounds, all of them, yet also strange and distant; but he knew that it was he that was different.

In his living-room, he poured whisky, drank it. Lit a cigarette, and heaved the smoke greedily into his lungs ... then he remembered the sedative tablets. He took them out, stared at them in his hand, then, with a quick movement, tossed them into his mouth. They stuck in his throat ...

Gagging, he ran into the kitchen, filled a glass with water and washed them down.

Back in the living-room, he drank more whisky. After a while he took the framed photo of Tania and Peter from the mantelpiece, sat down and stared at it.

'How did it all happen?' he whispered. 'How could it have happened ...?'

The photo slipped from his fingers on to the floor. He curled, foetus-like, on the sofa, and at last began crying. Another part of him thought, *I can't bear it,* although he knew he'd have to. After a while, the pills and whisky did their work, and he slid into unconsciousness.

At a quarter to nine the next morning, he telephoned the police from the laboratory and told them that he had just killed Richard Kelso there.

5

I wouldn't care to put a price on her, Tom thought as he came into Marcus Evans's office at the Department of Health the following Tuesday.

'Have a seat, Tom,' Marcus said. 'This is Mrs Sheila Castleton—she's Unit General Manager of Regis Hospital Trust in Dorset. Mrs Castleton, Mr Tom Jones.'

'How d'you do?' Tom said politely.

'Hello.' She was sitting a little to one side of Marcus's desk—blonde, with shoulder pads, a Just So hair style and vivid blue eyes. Tom put her at about fifty.

Marcus continued, 'I think it might be best if I briefly recap what you've told me, Mrs Castleton, for Mr Jones's benefit.'

'Very well.'

He turned to Tom. 'Three days ago, last Saturday, a scientific officer at the microbiology lab at Regis Hospital rang the police to say that he'd just killed one of his colleagues there. When the police arrived, they found him, together with his colleague's body. He'd apparently been strangled.

'After he'd been taken into custody, he

64

told them a strange story. Apparently, his baby son had died at the hospital the night before and he claimed that his colleague, whom he'd just killed, had deliberately put a false lab result into the hospital computer system, so that the boy received the wrong treatment.'

'Blimey,' said Tom.

'Not an easy one to get your mind around, is it? Anyway, he then went on to say—'

'Excuse me,' said Mrs Castleton, leaning forward, 'but I can't help wondering whether Mr Jones might find it easier to follow if he knew their names.' She turned to him. 'Harry Benedict killed Richard Kelso.'

'You're quite right, of course,' agreed Marcus, who'd just come to the same conclusion himself. 'Thank you.' He turned back to Tom. 'Benedict told the police that he'd driven into the lab to look at the test results, because he couldn't understand why his son had died. Kelso, who was already there, attacked him, and in the ensuing fight, Benedict killed him in self-defence.'

'Were there any witnesses?'

'No.'

'Then he's got a problem.'

'Indeed he has—the police have charged him with murder. However, when the police arrived, Benedict showed them that the test itself, and the result pencilled on the request form, were different from that in the computer.'

'So Kelso *had* put in the wrong result?'

'No—well, not at first, anyway. At this point, the hospital computer people were brought in, and they found that Kelso had put in the *right* result, the one pencilled on the form. However, within the next minute, *somebody* had changed this to the wrong result.'

'Didn't the computer record the passwords?'

'Both results bear Kelso's password.'

'Did he have a motive for harming the boy?'

'Apparently he and Benedict couldn't stand the sight of each other.'

'What do the police think?'

'They think that Kelso *did* change the result which seems rather odd when they've charged Benedict with his murder.'

'It's routine,' said Tom. 'They always go for the highest charge, because they can accept a lesser one later if the facts warrant it.'

'Anyway, that's the story,' said Marcus. He looked over at Mrs Castleton again. 'Would that be a fair summing-up?'

'Yes,' she said. 'A very lucid summary.'

'Thank you.'

She turned to Tom. 'The Trust's problem, Mr Jones, is not whether Benedict killed Kelso in self-defence—that's not our concern. We want to see justice done, of course,' she added hastily, 'but that's a matter for the police and the courts.'

Peter's inquest, she explained, would be followed by an enquiry at which the Trust would be asked some very awkward questions, to wit: Could this death have been avoided? Were the Trust culpable? Had they taken all practicable steps to ensure that it couldn't happen again?

'To do that,' she continued, 'we not only have to be certain that it was Kelso who did it, but to know exactly *what* it was he did. Why, for instance, did he put the true result in first, and why did he leave it pencilled on the path form?'

'Of course, he's not around any more to answer those questions himself,' said Tom thoughtfully, looking at her with a bit more respect.

'No,' she agreed. 'Which means that there will always be a question mark over his guilt. And if by some chance it wasn't him, then we'll be asked how it was that our new computer system, recently installed at great expense for the improvement of patient care, could be so easily subverted?'

'The computer as murder weapon,'

mused Tom. 'Yes, the tabloids'll love it.'

'Don't,' she said with a delicate shudder.

'I take it there's no doubt that the result *was* deliberately altered?'

'None whatever.'

'So, basically, you want to know who altered it?'

'We're perfectly happy—no, that's the wrong word.' She took a breath. 'Our computer department is satisfied that Kelso put in the false result immediately after putting in the right one, thinking that the change wouldn't be noticed and that the whole thing could be passed off as a mistake.'

'Surely not,' said Tom. 'I mean, the boy did die.'

'I don't understand it either, Mr Jones—you'll have to speak to them about it. Our problem is that even if this was, as we believe, the random act of an individual madman, we can't be seen to declare our own house in order.'

'No ...'

'We must have independent confirmation that Kelso was responsible. Of course, we'll then be asked how such an unstable person was allowed to do such sensitive work, but that'll be the Microbiology Service's problem.'

Tom said, 'You can make a computer

system foolproof, but it's virtually impossible to make it villain-proof—if the villain also happens to be a password holder.'

'Yes, and we'd obviously prefer that Kelso was the villain—because if someone else has compromised our system, there's nothing to stop them doing it again.'

'But from what you say, that's pretty unlikely.'

'Yes, but we need to show that it's impossible.'

Tom smiled. 'Impossible's a very big word.'

'I think perhaps we've gone as far as we can for the moment,' Marcus interposed. 'Apart from anything else, we ought to make sure we know where we are with the police.'

She turned to him. 'As I told you earlier, Mr Evans, the police are aware that I was coming here.' She hesitated. 'I hope you can appreciate that there is an element of urgency.'

'I'll speak to them in a moment and then let you know what we decide.'

'In that case, I won't take up any more of your time.'

Marcus settled Mrs Castleton in the coffee lounge, then rejoined Tom.

'You didn't like her much, did you?' Tom said. Like Marcus, he spoke with a

69

distinct London accent, only more so.

'Not much, no. Probably just me being old-fashioned and sexist, but she is a bit of an ice madam, isn't she?'

'Perhaps you have to be to manage a hospital trust.'

'Perhaps you do,' Marcus agreed. He was wearing his usual dark suit, accentuating his pale skin, billiard-ball head and heavy black moustache. Tom was more casually dressed in leather jacket and light-coloured trousers, although he was wearing a tie.

'How d'you feel about it?' Marcus asked.

Tom shrugged. 'Surely it's a matter for the police and the hospital computer department?'

'You heard her, they need independent confirmation.'

'There're plenty of independent computer consultants around.'

'I want you to do this one, Tom.'

'Why? I mean, it's not really our remit, is it?'

Marcus's department had been set up some years before to investigate the sort of serious fraud in the NHS that for one reason or another was outside the jurisdiction of the police.

'I think it is,' Marcus said. 'It was the phrase you used earlier—*the computer as murder weapon*. More and more hospital functions are being taken over by computers, and it's a trend that's going to continue—you know that as well as I do. The general public is uneasy enough as it is about all their personal details being held on computer, and if it gets out that one was used to commit an unsolved murder, there'll be a furore. I want you to either confirm that it was Kelso, or find out who did do it.'

'But with Kelso, dead,' Tom, protested, 'it's going to be virtually impossible to prove anything.'

'I'm not sure that legal proof matters, so long as you can find out exactly what happened and tell them how they can stop it happening again.'

'But there's no guarantee I could do even that ... OK, OK, I'll do it,' he capitulated, seeing the look on Marcus's face. 'At least I won't need any cover this time.' He looked up. 'What could make someone deliberately kill someone else's child?'

'God knows.'

Marcus, looking back at him, reflected how Tom's attitude to life had mellowed since the birth of his own son; even the contours of his musteline face seemed a little less unforgiving—and, at last, his hair had begun to go grey at the temples. *Although he'll probably die with a full head of the stuff,* he thought sourly. 'Well,' he said, 'I'd better tackle the police.'

Superintendent Southey of the Dorset Constabulary had a loud voice, loud enough to make Marcus hold the receiver a little way from his ear, so that Tom could hear the irritation without catching any of the words.

'I think I'd have to insist on that, Superintendent,' Marcus said, a hint of tungsten entering his voice. Tom pricked his ears.

'I don't think you need worry about that. Mr Jones was in the Metropolitan Police himself for some years, so I know he'll be sensitive to your concerns.'

Since when did being an ex-copper qualify you in sensitivity? Tom wondered.

Marcus looked up at him. 'Tom—two o'clock tomorrow afternoon?'

Tom nodded.

'That'll be fine, superintendent ... Yes, goodbye, and thanks for your help.'

'What did you have to insist on?' Tom asked as Marcus replaced the phone.

'He didn't want to let you see any of the witness statements. He's worried about confidentiality, so you'd better use some of that sensitivity I credited you with.'

They told Mrs Castleton their decision, and then she rang Dr Crowe to arrange for Tom to interview the lab staff. Crowe

72

wasn't very happy, but agreed to see Tom on Thursday.

'When it comes down to it,' Marcus observed, 'he doesn't have much choice.'

'That's a moot point,' said Mrs Castleton. 'As I mentioned to you earlier, he's not a Trust employee and he does rather tend to value his independence.'

'He still doesn't have much choice,' Marcus said quietly. His clout was of the quiet variety.

Holly Jones always worried when Tom had to go away—overtly, for his safety, and covertly, about what he might be up to out of her sight—so when he told her about this job, she felt both relieved and slightly cheated. Relieved that it wasn't likely to be dangerous, cheated because she had to keep her other worries to herself.

'How long d'you think you'll be away?' she asked. 'Oh, Hal, *no!*' She was spooning food for their sixteen-month-old son and he'd just spat a mouthful on to the floor.

'I won't have much idea till I get there,' Tom said.

Holly held out a plastic cup for Hal, which he grabbed and sucked at with alacrity. 'What do you say, Hal?'

''K yoo.'

'You're welcome.' She turned back to Tom. 'You did say Regis-on-Sea microbiology lab?'

'Yes.'

'I think I know someone who works there.'

'Really? Who?'

'Remember that immunology course I went on when I was pregnant? I met her there—Amina Khatoon.'

'Cartoon?'

'No, *Kha*toon,' she said crossly, and spelt it. 'It's Asian.'

Holly had a musical Devonian accent that was somehow all one with her attractive squarish face, and Tom still pretended to misunderstand it whenever he could.

'I was paired with her for the practical work and we got to know each other quite well.'

'Is she still there, d'you know?'

'I think so, she was when I last heard from her.'

'What's she like?'

'Very pretty, graceful. A bit secretive, though. She didn't tell me until the last day that her father had disowned her for having an English boyfriend.'

'He had other plans for her, I suppose?'

'Yes. She'd been chucked out of home and was still a bit shocked by it.'

'Hardly surprising. Did she end up happy ever with the boyfriend?'

'I don't think so. She still sends a Christmas card and I think she'd have mentioned it.'

'Is she bright?'

'Oh, very. Single-minded, too. Determined.'

'Observant?'

Holly looked at him sharply. 'Why? I hope you're not thinking of involving her, Tom.'

'No ... it's just that if she's as bright as you say, and observant, I'll be very interested in what she has to say, that's all.'

6

At twenty past two the next day, Tom sat waiting in Regis Central Police Station, wondering if there was any correlation between waiting time and the status of he-who-waits, or whether he was just being put in his place ...

The mood of the gods had improved since Friday; sea, sand and sky looked as though they'd been washed clean and a scattering of late holiday-makers speckled the beach like confetti.

Tom had booked into his hotel, a gull-stained Victorian pile on the seafront a hundred yards or so from the pier, then set out on foot for the police station.

He'd stayed in Regis once as a boy, but had forgotten (if he'd ever noticed) the maze of narrow streets and alleyways behind the façade of the seafront that echoed, almost like a Cornish fishing village, to the cries of scavenging gulls. One of these looked up hopefully at Tom as he passed before returning its attention to a discarded chip wrapping. The police station was near the harbour, a sixties building that sat uncomfortably despite a recent face-lift.

He looked up as a door opened and a secretary put her head through. 'Mr Jones? Superintendent Southey will see you now.'

He followed her through a noisy, open-plan office, where policemen did battle with their typewriters and policewomen tried persuasion on theirs, then along a narrow corridor. She tapped on the door at the end, then pushed it open at the incoherent grunt from within.

'Mr Jones, superintendent.'

'Thanks, Maggie—come in, Mr Jones. Oh, Maggie—could you ask Inspector Kendall to spare us a few minutes, please?'

Southey had half risen as Tom approached him, and now perfunctorily shook his hand and indicated one of the chairs in front of his desk. 'I understand you want to look into the computer aspects of Peter Benedict's death?'

'That's right.'

'Well, that's all right by me, so long as your enquiry doesn't interfere with ours.'

Tom studied him briefly before replying. He was a tallish man, slim, with thinning sandy hair and a military moustache, and Tom thought he looked rather jaded.

'I certainly don't want to interfere with your enquiry,' he said mildly, 'but I'll have to talk to the same people as you.'

'Some perhaps, but I thought your enquiries were concerned with recommending changes to the computer system.'

'To do that properly, superintendent. I must know exactly what happened.'

'But isn't that why you're here, so that I can tell you?'

Marcus's call obviously still rankled and he was the whipping boy, Tom realised. *Is this where I'm supposed to be sensitive but firm?* he wondered.

Then Southey said, 'I've prepared a summary for you. I think you'll find it covers everything you need to know.' He swallowed. 'I've also photocopied the relevant witness statements. I'm trusting you to treat them in confidence.'

'That goes without saying,' Tom said gratefully.

'We'll go through the summary then, shall we? I've made a copy of that as well.' He held it out, donned a pair of gold-framed spectacles and cleared his throat.

'The 999 call was received from Mr Benedict on Saturday 3rd September at 0846 hours and a patrol car arrived at the laboratory five minutes later. In the entrance hall was a body, which Benedict said was that of Richard Kelso.'

Southey held out a photo. It showed a bearded figure lying on its side at the foot of a flight of stairs. The eyes were still open and seemed to be staring in surprise at something above the photographer's head. Tom studied it for a moment, then handed it back.

He'd been declared dead by the police doctor, Southey continued, and the body photographed and removed. By this time, the lab staff had started arriving for the Saturday shift; they'd been held in the rest room while Harry took the officers upstairs and showed them some test plates, a path form and a computer result. He'd then been brought to the station for questioning, where he'd told them about Peter.

'The next morning, his son's death, in his own words, didn't make sense to him, so he drove to the laboratory to look at the tests himself.' Southey looked up. 'I'll read you the next part of his statement, since it speaks so vividly for itself.' He found it and cleared his throat again.

'"When I got there, I saw Richard Kelso's car parked outside. I don't know how long it had been there. I went inside. Richard Kelso was on the stairs. I don't know whether he had been going up or coming down. When he saw me, he shouted: 'You bastard,' and attacked me. We fought. I had my hands round his neck. I was trying to push him away but he kept hitting me. Suddenly, he went completely slack. I tried to revive him, then realised he was dead. I then rang the ambulance and police. While I was waiting for them, I went upstairs to look at my son's test results. I discovered that the test itself and the result pencilled on the form were different from the result in the computer, which was the one used to treat my son."'

He was right, Tom thought, it did speak vividly. What would *he* have done if it had been *his* son? The same, he supposed.

Southey said: 'The PM report indicates that Kelso died from vagal inhibition, resulting from the fracture of the hyoid bone—I imagine you've come across that before?'

Tom nodded. 'Manual strangulation fractures the hyoid bone here—' he indicated under his chin—'which breaks the vagus nerve, and the resulting shock causes heart failure.'

'Exactly. Then you'll also realise that this is in complete accordance with Benedict's story. In fact, nothing we've found so far contradicts it.'

'So it could have been accidental death, and/or self-defence.'

'Between you and me, the worst he'll be convicted of is manslaughter. Officially, we've charged him with murder and we're waiting to see what the Crown Prosecution Service have to say.'

'Is he out on bail?'

'Released yesterday. We've got his passport, of course, and he's been ordered to keep away from the press and the hospital.'

He paused while Tom made a note, then told him how they'd shown the evidence to Dr Crowe, who'd said that while it was obvious *now* that the wrong result had been entered into the computer, it could have originally occurred through a genuine mistake. 'Apparently, he'd known Peter was ill—he'd been consulted about it and had recommended that the wrong treatment be maintained, because the spurious computer result was all he had to go by. He felt pretty sick about that.'

'I can imagine,' Tom said.

They'd then spoken to Chris Parker, the hospital's computer boss, Southey continued, and it was he who discovered that there had been no mistake, that the *correct* result had been input at 1735 that evening and the *wrong* one substituted at 1736. Both results had been under Richard's password.

'Is password security tight, d'you know?' Tom asked.

'They say so. Besides, the timings make it virtually impossible for anyone else to have done it, even if they *had* known Kelso's password.'

'Did anyone actually see Kelso putting them in?'

'I was just coming to that,' Southey said testily. He explained where everybody had been at the time, how Joy and Amina had both seen Richard working on the test, but not the computer. 'It's all there in the statements.'

Tom thought for a moment. 'What about Kelso's motive, are you happy with that?'

'Yes. It's generally agreed that he'd loathed Benedict for some time. Apparently, Peter's mother had once been engaged to him and he'd never forgiven Benedict for taking her away—especially since she'd subsequently died.'

'Oh?' Tom looked up. 'How did that happen?'

'Car accident—nothing suspicious about it.' He went on to tell Tom how their mutual loathing had led to the fight that afternoon.

Tom looked out of the window for a moment, then back at Southey. 'But is that really motive enough to deliberately kill someone else's child?'

'I know what you mean,' Southey said bleakly. 'One thing I am sure of is that he did it on the spur of the moment. The fight must have just pushed him over the edge, so that when the opportunity to do him harm suddenly arose ...' He shrugged.

'What about the staff on the ward, didn't they notice anything unusual?'

'Inspector Kendall handled that side of things.' Southey glanced up at the clock on the wall. 'I'd have thought she'd be here by now. However ...' He turned over a page. 'Peter hadn't responded to treatment and at about 1725, Dr—er—Miller asked the lab to read the antibiotic tests early as a matter of urgency.

'Kelso phoned the ward sometime between 1735 and 1740—nobody seems to know the exact time because the sister wasn't there and they were in a panic. Anyway, Kelso told them that the results were in the computer, and Dr Miller started the new, and as we now know, wrong treatment—'

He was interrupted by a light knock on the door.

'Come in,' he called. The door opened and an elegantly dressed woman of about thirty hurried in.

'Sorry, sir, I've been interviewing.' She was breathless, slightly flushed. 'The Chambers case.' Her face was full, almost classical, with dark blonde hair worn up, and Tom's eyes were immediately drawn to her.

Southey smiled indulgently at her. 'That's all right, Liz. Any luck?'

'I think so ...'

'Tell me about it later. Liz, this is Mr Jones from the Department of Health. Mr Jones, Inspector Kendall.'

Tom was already on his feet, holding out his hand. 'Hello.'

They sat down again and Southey explained why Tom was there. Tom found his eyes roving her face—a strong face, but entirely feminine—almost tasting it and the dark honey hair above ... She glanced at him and he looked away.

Southey was saying, 'Actually, Mr Jones, I think we'd just about finished. D'you have any questions?'

He brought himself to order and glanced through the summary. 'Let's see if I've got the gist of it ... Kelso has always hated Benedict and has a fight with him on Friday. Later, he reads Peter Benedict's antibiotic test, puts the *right* result into the computer, more or less immediately changes it to the *wrong* result, and then rings the ward and tells them it's in the computer. Peter is given the wrong treatment and dies.'

'Yes, I think that covers it—wouldn't you agree, Liz?'

'Er—yes, sir.'

Tom, noticing the slight hesitation, decided to probe.

'I wonder *why* he put the right result in first,' he mused. 'If he was going to do it, why not do it straight away?'

'Because, as I told you earlier, it was done on the spur of the moment,' said Southey.

'Didn't the screen show that there'd been a change?'

'Liz?' Southey redirected the question.

She turned her eyes on Tom, deep brown eyes. 'Not as it happens, no. It was an unauthorised result—I expect you already know what that means?'

'One not officially approved as the final result.'

'Yes, and as such, it was not only easier to change, but there was also no record of it on the screen. We didn't realise it had been changed ourselves until we got the computer people to look into it.' Her voice was low and clear with no discernible accent.

'Inspector Kendall has a better understanding of computers than I,' Southey said, unnecessarily.

'So, is it possible,' Tom asked her, 'that without Benedict's intervention, the whole thing could have been passed off as an accident?'

'We think so, yes. If Kelso hadn't been killed, nobody else would have realised that the result had been changed. It would have been put down to human error.'

'Then I wonder why Kelso, having realised that, left the correct result pencilled on the path form.'

'Because he forgot in the heat of the moment,' Southey said irritably. 'He remembered the next morning and that's why he went back to the lab—to destroy it. But he was interrupted by Benedict.'

Tom nodded slowly. 'That certainly fits. If it did happen that way, Superintendent, then the murder charge against Benedict isn't worth very much.'

'That's for a court to decide, Mr Jones.'

'What's your guess about Peter's inquest?'

'I think you'll find that Kelso killed him.' He smiled grimly. 'He may be

85

beyond the law courts now, but he can still be found guilty by the Coroner.'

'So, in effect, he got what he deserved?'

'Those are your words, Mr Jones,' Southey said deliberately. 'So far as I'm concerned, justice is not for privatisation and Benedict's fate must be decided by a court of law.' He glanced up at the clock—by now, it was nearly three. 'If there's nothing else, I do have another appointment shortly.'

'And I have to go and see the computer people.' Tom closed his notebook and got to his feet. 'Thanks for your help, Superintendent—and you, inspector. Oh, if I find anything unexpected, or need to speak to you again ...?'

Southey had stood as well. 'I think it might be best if you liaised with Inspector Kendall, especially since she's so much more *au fait* with computers than me.'

Suits me, thought Tom.

7

If asked, Tom would say that he didn't care greatly for hospitals. This was an understatement; he detested them, which was unfortunate, since he had to spend so much of his time in them. *It's the money*, he told himself as the glass doors of Regis General's new main entrance hissed smoothly aside. *I do it for the money.*

He found himself in a large, airy foyer of brick and glass with a shining chequered floor. He cautiously sniffed the air as he approached the enquiries desk, but couldn't detect any of the usual hospital smells.

He was directed to the admin block and ten minutes later was closeted with Chris Parker, head of the computer department, a cheerful, skinny extrovert with a bony face and prominent Adam's apple.

'I can show you Peter Benedict's file straight away if you like,' he said, 'but I thought it might help if I first showed you exactly how Richard Kelso changed the result.'

'OK,' said Tom.

'We use the Combined Hospital System here.' He tapped the letters CHS into the terminal in front of him and a colourful logo appeared, followed by a prompt. 'It's a commercial package, quite flexible, with some good points, some not so good.'

'About par for the course, then?'

'Yeah,' Parker agreed. 'I've set up a dummy patient record.' His long fingers rattled the keyboard. 'Here we are ...'

'Joseph Bloggs,' observed Tom. 'An

87

original choice—and you've given him piles, I see.'

'It seemed appropriate,' Parker said.

Tom couldn't see how, but didn't ask. Parker flitted through the screens until he came to the microbiology program, then turned back to Tom. 'Imagine I'm Kelso putting in the result ...' He keyed in R for resistant against one of the antibiotics, then came out of the program and logged off.

'Now, I decide to change it.' He logged on again using the same password, found the program and substituted an S. 'The system allows me to do that,' he said, 'because the results haven't been authorised yet.'

'And there's nothing on the screen to show that it's been changed,' said Tom.

'No,' agreed Parker. 'Perhaps there ought to be,' he added thoughtfully.

'Some of the systems I've seen also require an extra code word before you can make a change like that, even on an unauthorised result.'

'I've always found it better to rely on password access levels,' Parker said defensively. 'Besides—' a hint of desperation entered his voice—'it wouldn't have made any difference in this case, would it? I mean, if a bona fide password holder suddenly decides to do something like this, there's not a lot we can do about it, is there?'

'No,' agreed Tom. 'Not if it was Kelso who did it.'

'Did you say *if* ... ?'

Tom smiled. 'Let's have a look at Peter Benedict's record now, shall we?'

'All right.' Parker put an end to Joseph Bloggs's suffering by erasing his record, then logged on again with his own password and called up Peter's.

'This record is evidence, so Mrs Castleton and I are the only people who can access it now.'

COMBINED HOSPITAL SYSTEM
PATIENT RECORD

SET UP BY: Miss K. Ashfield DATE:
[220995] TIME: [0950]
HOSPITAL NUMBER [R21603]
SURNAME BENEDICT
FIRST NAME PETER

'Let's have a look at the Patient Notes,' Parker said. 'Normally, only senior ward staff could access this.'

PATIENT NOTES Dr N Miller DATE:
[220995] TIME: [1031]
0935 Patient arrived in considerable
    distress

Prelim. exam of ear: Inflammation +++
Discharge +++
? Otitis Externa Requested urgent Gram
stain
1945 Temp 39.1 Paracetamol suppository
Gram stain suggests staphylococcal infection
1015 Commenced IV Flucloxacillin

'You'd probably find more detail than that in the written notes on the ward,' Parker said. 'They often just transcribe a summary on to the computer.'

He flicked through the screens until he reached the last one.

2055 Temp 40.1 Telephoned Dr Crowe
—maintain Gentamicin
2155 Temp 40.6 Telephoned Dr Crowe
—2205 transferred to ITU. Clindamycin, Vancomycin, on ventilator.
2230 Dopamine
0003 Death
Dr E Whittaker [230995] [0017]

Although Tom hadn't known him, or even seen a photo of him, the sight of this record, in a sense all that was left of Peter Benedict, made him blink and swallow.

'As you can see—' Parker's voice was quieter now— 'the record was set up when he was admitted and the doctors and nursing staff entered the details throughout

the day until he died.' He let out a sigh.
'Makes you hope there's a heaven, doesn't
it? You got any kids?'

'One. A boy, about the same age as this
one. How about you?'

'Two girls, older. Makes you think a bit
more about them, though.'

'Yeah,' Tom agreed. After a pause, he
said, 'Can we look at the microbiology
results now?'

'Sure.' He pressed some more keys and
the screen was replaced with another:

LABORATORY INVESTIGATIONS
Set up by: Miss A Khatoon [220995]
[0946]
PRELIMINARY GRAM STAIN
Gram Positive Cocci in clumps +++
Pus cells +++

Mr R Kelso [220995] [1736]
*** Direct Sens read 1730 at urgent
request of Dr N Miller

Penicillin	R		Fucidin	S
Ampicillin	R		Vancomycin	S
Flucloxacillin	R		Tetracycline	S
Clindamycin	S	Chloramphenicol		S
Gentamicin	S	Erythromycin		R

'That's the amended—*false*, I should
say—result. Now let's have a look at
what Mr R Kelso put in the first time

91

...' He tapped some more keys.

There were just three differences: the time, 1735; the appendage BACKUP; and an R instead of an S against Gentamicin.

'Such a tiny change,' Parker said. 'An S for an R—that's all it took to kill him.'

'No chance it was some sort of computer malfunction?'

'None at all—the system simply isn't capable of making a mistake like that. That alteration was made deliberately and maliciously.' His voice was scarred with anger.

'The question is,' Tom said, 'by whom?'

'Oh, it has to be Kelso.'

'Why?'

Parker took a breath. 'To explain that, I'll have to tell you how the password system works here.'

'OK.'

'Every user has a personal code that never changes. For instance, Kelso's was K201, because he was the two hundred and first member of staff in the region whose name began with K.'

Tom nodded.

'When a user logs on to the computer,' Parker continued, 'they put in this number, followed by their own secret password. Kelso's was BITCH, which makes you wonder about his state of mind.'

'It does rather, doesn't it?' agreed

Tom. 'So, he'd put in K201, followed by BITCH.'

'That's right. The idea is that if some other warped personality chose BITCH as their password, they could still be differentiated by the code. D'you follow?'

'Mm. I imagine the staff change their passwords fairly often?'

'They have to—after two months, the computer tells them to change it and won't accept the old one.'

'How long had Kelso had BITCH?'

'A month.'

'In which time, someone could have seen him using it.'

'I sincerely hope not,' Parker said with some asperity. 'I went over and lectured them myself on the importance of password security when they had the system installed.'

'But supposing someone else *did* know it—what's to have prevented them changing the result?'

'The timings of the two results—1735 and 1736. That second result was put in immediately after the first—who else could have known exactly when to do it?'

Tom said slowly. 'You know, in theory, it needn't have been done quite immediately. If the clock had *just* changed to 1735 when Kelso put the first result in, there could have been anything up to a two-minute gap.'

'Yeah, and if it had been just about to change, it would have been two seconds.'

'All right,' Tom conceded with a smile. 'But there *were* others in the building at the time, weren't there?'

'They'd have to have known Kelso's personal code, his password, and exactly when he'd put the first result in.'

'Mm.' Tom thought for a moment. 'If someone did know all that, could it have been done anywhere other than the lab?'

'In theory it could have been done anywhere in the region, since the computer doesn't record the terminal being used ... maybe it should do that as well,' he said, thoughtful again. 'But the timings make it virtually impossible.'

'OK, but it *could* have been someone in the lab other than Kelso, if they'd known his code, his password and when he put the first result in?'

Parker shrugged. 'Under those circumstances, yes.' He looked at Tom quizzically. 'Do you really think that's a possibility?'

'Not really, no—but I've got to look at it as though I do.' He paused. 'One thing does bother me a bit—people have told me that the whole thing could have been passed off as an accident, but Kelso must have realised that if the boy died and there

94

was an enquiry, suspicion would be bound to fall on him.'

'Yes, but it would have looked like a genuine mistake. You see, they'd only have that second result—if they hadn't involved me, they wouldn't have known it had been changed. And if Kelso hadn't been killed, they probably wouldn't have involved me.' He sighed as his eyes met Tom's. 'That program's going to have to be redesigned, isn't it?'

8

When he got back to the hotel, Tom made some coffee, went through all the statements Southey had given him, then phoned Marcus.

'Not much doubt so far as officialdom's concerned, then?' Marcus said when Tom finished.

'Not really, no.'

'Keep looking, Tom. I want no doubts at all.'

'Yessir ...'

He rang off, phoned Holly, exchanged a few gurgles with Hal and then looked at his watch.

A quarter to six—it wouldn't be dark

for an hour or two, so he had time to look around before dinner.

He went down to his car, an elderly but immaculate Mini Cooper, studied his map and then set off for Maidenswell, where Richard Kelso had lived, following the route he assumed Kelso would normally have taken. It was about five miles.

Once he was free of the suburbs, the soft Dorset flora seemed to gather around him, as though sharing an intimacy. The shallow valley he was following was dotted with trees, mostly oak, and the late summer gloss of their leaves seemed to capture the evening light, hold and softly glow with it.

Maidenswell was a secretive place of grey stone and thatch. Tom found Kelso's cottage near the centre of the village and stopped the car for a moment. It was one of those buildings that look as though they've grown out of the soil rather than having been merely built on it.

Not short of a Euro or two, he thought.

He looked at his map again and saw that Broadwell, where Harry Benedict lived, was only a mile or so away. He drove over and found the address.

Benedict obviously wasn't so well off as Kelso had been; Broadwell was more a sprawling dormitory than a village and his house was an end-of-terrace that an

96

estate agent might have called a cottage, but wasn't in the same league as Kelso's. A blue Ford Escort stood in the driveway. Lights were on and, for a moment, Tom wondered about calling, then decided to stick with the order of interviews he'd already worked out. He turned the car round and drove back the way he'd come.

Another car was coming towards him, a police car, and as he pulled in to let it pass, he saw that Liz Kendall was driving.

He raised a hand in greeting and wound down his window. She stopped and there was a buzz as she lowered hers.

'Hello, Inspector.'

'Mr Jones. Fancy meeting you here.' Her voice was cool, but not unfriendly. 'You certainly don't waste any time.'

'I haven't spoken to him yet—I was just getting to know the topography.'

'Ah. Well, I do have to speak to him, so I'd better be going.' She reached for the window button.

'Can I buy you a drink?' Tom said on impulse. 'After you've seen him. The superintendent did say we were to liaise,' he added.

She looked askance at him for a moment, then said, 'All right.'

'The local pub here?'

'No.' She shook her head. 'Not the local pub here. If you really know the topography, you'll be able to find the Fleet in Maidenswell. I'll see you there in about twenty minutes.' She raised the window and drove on.

Tom drove back to Maidenswell. He found a pub called the George, but no sign of the Fleet. Eventually, he asked a venerable worthy, who directed him down a back lane so narrow he hadn't noticed it before.

The Fleet was an austere building of uneven stone. He parked, walked inside and down a flagstoned corridor. To the right was a dining-room, empty; to the left a bar, the only one, so far as he could see.

He went in. There were perhaps half a dozen people clustered round it, who stopped talking as soon as they saw him. He nodded, said, 'Evening.'

'Evenin',' one of them muttered back.

His eye was caught by a wooden cask on trestles with the legend 'Goliath' stamped on it and he ordered a pint. It gurgled satisfyingly out of the tap. He took it over to a table and sat down.

She probably thought I'd never find it and kissed off home, he thought gloomily. He tried the beer. It was beautiful.

The locals had started talking again, so he lit a cheroot and extended an ear, listening to the accent as much as to what they were saying. It was softer than that of Holly's home in Devon, but still unmistakably West of England.

He'd finished the cheroot and most of the beer when Liz Kendall walked in.

He stood up. 'What can I get you?'

'Oh, a half of what you're drinking, please. I'm off duty,' she added with a grin.

The locals went into their silent routine again while he bought her drink and another pint for himself. As he returned to her, she said, 'We'll take them outside, shall we?'

He followed her down the passage and into a courtyard where a few hens were scratching about. 'We were cramping their style,' she said to him. 'Anyway, it's nicer out here.' She walked on to a small and not very exciting garden—except for the view.

'Blimey,' Tom said.

The land fell away from them down to the sea in a series of hills so perfect, so entire in themselves it seemed they must have been sculpted. *They're feminine,* he thought, *those hills are feminine.*

'Is that Chesil Beach?' he asked her after a moment.

She was swallowing a mouthful of Goliath. 'Thirsty,' she said. Then, 'Yes, that's Chesil Beach.'

The thin bank of shingle a mile or so below ran roughly parallel to the coast, separating a long stretch of water from the rest of the sea, before fading into the haze either side. The sea beat creamily against it.

'The water this side's called the Fleet,' she added.

'Thus the name of the pub,' said Tom. 'Is there any way in for a boat?'

'Only over the shingle.'

They stood a few moments more looking down through the hills on to the flat water, the low sun and livid gash of its reflection, then she moved over to one of the benches.

'Mission accomplished?' Tom asked as he joined her. 'With Mr Benedict.'

'Oh, it was only an amendment to his statement that needed signing.'

'How's he taking everything?'

She looked at him a moment as though pondering whether to answer. 'I'm no psychologist,' she said at last, 'but I wonder if he's really accepted it yet. He seems to be covering everything with a thick cloak of brashness—it's not particularly attractive, although I'm in no position to judge him. I imagine you'll make your own judgement when you meet him.'

'He's certainly had a bad enough time.' Tom drank some more beer. It *was* tasty, but on an empty stomach, it was making his head swim slightly. He said, 'I hadn't realised he'd lost his wife as well as his son.'

'They weren't married—they were living together.'

'I suppose the fact that they had a child made me think they were. Hopelessly old-fashioned,' he added.

'Yes,' she agreed.

He paused, knowing what he wanted to say but not sure how to. 'You've probably realised that so far as Mrs Castleton's concerned, the only reason I'm here is to cover her backside ...' *No, that's not right* ... 'What I'm trying to say is that I'm supposed to confirm your findings, and yet I had the feeling that you weren't quite so convinced about the case as the superintendent.'

She was smiling slightly at his discomfiture; looking at her, Tom realised that the classicality of her face was marred by the slightest excess of flesh beneath her chin, and yet somehow, he found this made her all the more attractive.

'I *think* I'm convinced,' she said. 'Everything points to it being Kelso. Except for the pencilled result on the path form.'

Tom nodded his head wisely, wished he hadn't. 'Have you raised it with his nibs?'

'He thinks it was an oversight in the heat of the moment, you heard him yourself this afternoon.'

'But you'd think that someone who'd just altered a computer result would also remember to alter what he'd written on the corresponding form. Wouldn't you?'

'Yes,' she agreed, 'I would, but he reminded me of how often killers do make stupid mistakes. He's convinced it's the reason Kelso went back to the lab.'

'What do *you* think?'

'I think he's right, but ...'

'There remains a niggle?'

'Yes ...' She hesitated. 'There was something else—it was me who interviewed the staff on the ward who took the phone message from Kelso, and there's something the super left out. When Kelso rang the ward, he asked—*demanded*, in fact—to speak to the sister. She'd been called away and one of the nurses had to go and look for her. When she came back—Sister Yate, that is—Kelso told her the results were in the computer, and then complained about the length of time he'd been kept waiting. Sister Yate says it can't have been more than a minute or two, but—'

'Wait a minute,' Tom interrupted. 'You're saying that Kelso made them go and find the sister, just to tell her that the results were in the computer?'

'Yes.'

'But that's crazy—why didn't he leave a message?'

'It does seem pretty daft—Sister Yate waxed quite lyrical about it. It's a new regulation, apparently because they've had problems with phoned messages. The thing is, there was a period of time when Kelso was on the phone, waiting to give the message. The super says it's irrelevant, because the computer timings show that he'd altered the result before he even picked up the phone. But it did make me wonder ...'

Tom said, 'Well, I realised something this afternoon as well ...' He told her how the computer timings could have meant anything up to a two-minute gap.

'So in theory,' Liz said, leaning forward, 'someone else could have changed that result while Kelso was waiting on the phone ...' The sun lit the down on one side of her face, turning it to gold, and he wanted to reach out and stroke it with the backs of his fingers.

'Er—yes.' He swallowed. 'Although they'd have to have known both Kelso's password and exactly when he'd put in the result.'

She leaned back again. 'Not very likely, is it?'

'It's a definite loophole, though.' He regarded her over his beer mug. 'I'll bear it in mind and have a good hard look at it.'

'Don't put too much weight on what I say, for goodness' sake. I'm sure the super's right—he's the one with the experience.' She drank some more of her own beer.

Listening to her, Tom realised that she did have a slight accent, the same as the locals in the bar. He said, 'D'you come from this area?'

'Yes.' She smiled. 'I was born in Regis Hospital, as a matter of fact.'

'How long have you been in the force?'

'Nearly ten years.'

'You've done well to make inspector.'

'Thanks.' She didn't attempt to deny it. 'I had to move around a bit, though.'

'But you came back?'

'Yes, I was lucky.' She paused. 'I understand you were in the police as well.'

'That's right, also for ten years.' He smiled back at her. 'I only made it as far as sergeant, though.'

'You time would have come,' she said, not patronisingly. 'What made you leave?'

He hesitated. 'To try and save my marriage.'

'Ah. Did it work? Leaving?'

He shook his head, and she said, 'It rarely does.'

'You've had a similar experience?'

It was her turn to hesitate. 'I did once have to decide between a relationship and my career, yes.'

Tom said, 'And although you made the *correct* decision, you find yourself wondering, even now, whether it was the right one.'

'How did you know?' she asked, her eyes on his face.

He shrugged.

She hesitated again, decided to continue. 'You see, I ran into him last week. He's married now, and to a career woman. And I wondered why it was that *we* couldn't manage it.'

'Perhaps you weren't suited in other ways?'

'I don't know, I thought we were at the time ... It was as though he wanted some tangible sign of my commitment to *him.*' She smiled, a twist of the lips. 'Perhaps he'd learned his lesson with me and wasn't going to risk it again.' She looked at him curiously. 'Why am I telling you all this?'

'Because we're strangers. And we've both been there, although we made different decisions.'

'D'you have any regrets?' she asked after another pause, 'About leaving the force?'

'No.'

'You don't miss being away from the sharp end of things?'

Tom suppressed a grin as he recalled some of the painfully blunt ends he'd experienced over the past few years, but contented himself with saying, 'Oh, my job has its moments.'

'Are you married now?'

'Yes,' he said after a microsecond's pause.

'Children?'

'One. A boy, about the same age as Peter Benedict.'

'Ah.'

'How d'you mean, *Ah?*'

'Oh, I don't know. I was wondering whether it made you feel personally involved, I suppose.'

'I don't think so. But it does somehow add a dimension to human frailty, doesn't it? In the sense that you can kill, or be killed, at the touch of a computer button.'

'Hasn't that been the case for years with nuclear weapons? *One push of the button* and so on?'

'Yes, but that's not the same thing.'

'Why not?'

'Because those sort of computers were designed to kill, in battle.' After the period of lucidity, he felt the fumes of Goliath returning. 'This computer is supposed to *save* lives.'

'I suppose so.' She finished the last of

her beer. 'Well, I must be going. Thanks for the drink—you don't have to get up.'

He wanted to say, *Please don't go yet,* but knew it would only be embarrassing, so he said, 'Thanks for your company—I enjoyed it. I expect we'll run into each other again.'

'I expect we will.'

He watched her go, then lit another cheroot and thought about her.

Despite Holly's misgivings, Tom loved his wife and was genuinely unsure of the nature of Liz's attraction for him. *What is it about her?* he wondered. *Sensuality without the sex ...? No, that's ridiculous. Some sort of resonance? ... Dream on, Tom ...* He thought about her as he watched the last chord of the sun sink slowly into the sea.

9

That'll be him ... Dr Theodore Crowe, watching from his window, didn't know quite *how* he knew, only that he *did* know as Tom's Mini Cooper drew up next to his Mercedes. *Looks half asleep to me,* he thought as the deceptively slight figure climbed out, locked the door and stood gazing for a moment at the entrance.

Tom was, in fact, half hungover. He'd missed dinner the night before and had made do with sandwiches; now, unease prowled his guts and a muzzy ache skulked behind his eyes.

Bloody Goliath, he thought. *Or Nemesis maybe, for my extramarital maunderings.*

He took a breath and went inside. The hall, dim after the sunlight, was of marble, as was the stairway to the upper storey. To one side was a hatch marked 'Reception'. He pressed the buzzer beside it and a young woman got up from a computer terminal. He explained who he was.

'If you'd like to take a seat,' she said, 'I'll tell Dr Crowe you're here.'

'Thanks.' He walked slowly over to the line of chairs and sat down.

Tom hated the smells of laboratories almost as much as those of hospitals. Disinfectants, ether, bodily exudates—all these recalled for him images of Frank, his haemophiliac brother, now dead after a long battle with AIDS; also his own blighted childhood and lifelong terror of the sight of blood. For a moment he actually had to fight the urge to get up and walk out ...

He dragged his mind back, thinking instead about what he was going to say. Dr Crowe probably wasn't going to welcome his speculations any more than Southey had, but what he'd learned from Parker and Liz Kendall did need looking into ... He smiled to himself as he thought about Liz—then the girl reappeared in front of him and said, 'Dr Crowe will see you now.'

Blimey! What does this say for my status?

He followed her up the stairs, their footsteps echoing slightly in the space around them. Crowe's office was slightly offset from the top of the stairway. She knocked.

'Come.'

She eased the door open. 'Mr Jones, Dr Crowe.'

'Come in, Mr Jones.' Crowe came from behind his desk and shook Tom's hand warmly, almost effusively. 'Have a seat.' He indicated some armchairs a little way from his desk. 'Would you like some coffee? I was about to have one.'

'Thank you, I will.' *It might deaden the smells ...*

'Two coffees, please, Yvonne,' Crowe said to the girl and she withdrew. Tom quickly glanced around the room as he sat down. It was spacious, airy and contained a large glass-fronted bookcase and small conference table as well as the ubiquitous computer terminal.

Crowe sat a chair away from him and

said, 'Well, Mr Jones, how can I help you? The sooner we can put this tragic business behind us, the better.'

He's a bit like Uncle Bill, Tom thought, taking in the honest, open face and pale blue eyes—*although I mustn't let that prejudice me.*

He explained his brief, keeping it as general as possible. 'I've already heard about the bad feeling between Kelso and Benedict.' He took out his notebook. 'How did that come about? What kind of people were—are they?'

There was a gentle knock on the door and Yvonne came in with a tray.

'On my desk please, Yvonne,' said Crowe.

After she'd gone, he got up and went over to the tray. 'Sugar?'

'Not for me, thanks.'

Crowe put three lumps in his own cup and brought them over. 'Where were we? Oh, yes—Harry and Richard and their mutual antipathy.' He sat down again, thoughtfully stirred his coffee.

They'd been two very distinct types, he told Tom—opposites, almost. Richard's father was a local builder and Richard had worked at the lab since he'd left school. He was quiet, slow, introverted, but reliable. 'What I'd call a technician, not a scientist,' he concluded, and Tom suppressed a smile as he remembered how Holly hated that description of her profession.

Harry had been completely different: he'd come from a poor background, but had a good science degree and wide experience.

'Why *did* he come here?' Tom asked. 'I don't mean to be rude, but if he was as well qualified as you suggest ...'

'He told me he wanted to get away from London. I thought he had genuine flair and would bring in some new ideas, new blood. I'm afraid I rather pressurised Joy, my laboratory manager, over him.' He looked away. 'I regret that now.'

'She didn't want to employ him?'

'No, and with hindsight, she was right—it was folly to imagine that someone like Harry would settle down here quietly with the rest of us ...' He tailed off.

'So there was trouble from the beginning?' Tom prompted.

No, Crowe told him, they'd got on tolerably well at first. Richard had just become engaged to Tania, who seemed to bring him out of himself, and everyone had been pleased for them.

'But Benedict had other plans?'

'Yes, although I don't think anything happened between them immediately. If you really want that sort of detail, I think Joy might be a better person to ask.'

Tom said, 'I'll do that, but for the moment, Dr Crowe, I'd like to hear your own recollections.'

Crowe's eyes flicked up at him. 'As you wish.'

'You were saying?' Tom cued him.

'I was saying, if you remember, that Joy was a better person to speak to about that kind of thing.'

Tom smiled. 'I accept that, Dr Crowe, but I'd still be interested to hear what you can remember.'

Crowe looked away again. 'I do remember that Harry acquired something of the reputation of a Lothario, although the only other name I can give you there is that of Amina Khatoon, another of our female staff.'

The English boyfriend ...?

'I do know that some people felt Harry treated Amina rather badly,' Crowe continued, 'although I wouldn't know the details myself. Anyway, some twenty months ago, Tania broke off the engagement and moved in with Harry. It was very sudden—overnight, almost. Richard was naturally very upset and they were enemies from there on.'

'They didn't call a truce when Tania was killed?'

'No, if anything, it had made things worse. It was a car accident, probably

112

Harry's fault, and Tania had been killed instantly, while Harry wasn't even scratched.'

'How long ago was this?' Tom asked.

Six or seven months, Crowe supposed. They'd all been surprised when Harry decided to stay on and his continued presence had exacerbated the bad feeling between the two of them.

'But was Kelso's hatred really so great,' Tom said, watching him, 'that he would deliberately kill Benedict's son?'

Crowe took a breath, released it. 'I'd never have believed it before,' he said at last. 'But now, I can see no alternative.'

'OK. Can we turn now to that Friday evening? You were here in the laboratory, I believe?'

'I was, yes, until about 6.30. There was an important report I had to have ready for Monday.'

'Can you remember who else was here?'

'Richard, Joy, and, I believe, Amina, although I didn't actually see her.'

'No one else?'

'Not that I know of.'

'Did you see Richard working on Peter's test at all?'

'No.'

Tom opened his case and brought out the computer printouts Parker had given him. 'I imagine you've already seen these?'

'I have indeed.'

'What strikes me is that only one antibiotic sensitivity was changed—this one here, Gentamicin.' He indicated it with his finger. 'How did Kelso, or whoever, know that this would be the antibiotic used?'

'Because with this sensitivity pattern, it's the drug of choice.'

'Why is that?'

Crowe explained why serious staph infections were usually treated with Flucloxacillin. 'When it became clear that this strain was resistant, an MRSA in fact, Dr Miller, correctly in my view, asked the lab to read the Direct Sensitivity test early. Given this pattern—' he tapped the altered result— 'Gentamicin is the most effective of the drugs available and therefore the automatic choice.'

'Is that something that's generally known?'

'Oh yes, anyone with a passing knowledge of clinical microbiology would know it.'

Tom made a note, then looked up. 'I know that you were consulted about Peter that evening—were you surprised that the Gentamicin hadn't worked?'

'Not at first, no—antibiotics do take time to work. By the time we realised that it wasn't going to, it was too late.'

'An MRSA you said—what is that?'

'In layman's terms, a multiple resistant *Staph. aureus*. They've evolved through

114

the overuse of antibiotics and are now a millstone round the neck of virtually every hospital in the land. Although we don't usually broadcast the fact,' he added.

'But Peter had this bug before he came to hospital, didn't he?'

'Yes, but Harry's a carrier and Peter almost certainly acquired it from him.'

Tom gazed at him incredulously. 'You're telling me that Harry Benedict actually carries this thing?'

'Oh yes, we've checked it out, he's a nasal carrier. But an awful lot of hospital workers are—some thirty per cent carry staphylococci without any ill effects to themselves.'

'I see,' said Tom slowly, not at all sure that he did. After a pause, he continued, 'How good would you say password security is here, Dr Crowe? Could anyone else have known Kelso's password?'

'I very much doubt it—the computer department here is very strict about password security.'

'OK. You mentioned just now that Benedict had treated Amina Khatoon badly—are there any others besides her who might've had a motive for wanting to harm him?'

Crowe took his time answering. 'Harry had his share of enemies,' he said at last, 'but I can't conceive of any who disliked him enough to want to harm his son.'

'But you do now think that of Richard Kelso?'

'Richard had become rather ... peculiar after Tania's death. I think that when he changed that result, the balance of his mind was quite literally disturbed. Were you aware that he'd physically attacked Harry that afternoon?'

'Were you a witness to that?'

'No.' Crowe shook his head. 'But Joy was—she had to break it up. Ask her.'

'I shall. But you said just now that Benedict had his share of enemies, and you mentioned Amina Khatoon—who were the others?'

Crowe regarded him steadily, his head a little to one side. 'Mr Jones, forgive me, but you do seem to be pressing this point rather. I did understand from the police that they weren't looking for any culprit other than Richard.' His earlier warmth had all but vanished.

'I've been asked to exclude the possibility of another culprit.'

'That wasn't made clear to me, either by yourself or Mrs Castleton.'

'I'm sorry if—'

Crowe cut in: 'I suppose in that case you'd have to include Joy Manners—she had no cause to love Harry either.'

'Why was that?' Tom asked quickly.

Crowe pursed his lips. 'Harry didn't suffer fools, or people he *considered* fools, gladly. He thought Joy a fool and she disliked him for it.'

'Was he justified?'

'Not to my mind. Joy may not be a high flyer technically, but she's a good manager. Harry has—had,' he corrected himself, 'an unfortunate habit of exposing her shortcomings and she quite naturally resented it.'

'Can you think of anyone else?'

'No. I'd have thought those I'd given you sufficient.'

Tom said, 'Why did you change tense just now, Dr Crowe? You said *had*, instead of *has*. Harry *had* an unfortunate habit ...'

Crowe considered him a moment before replying.

'I accept that Harry probably acted in self-defence when he killed Richard, although it will be for the courts to decide. However, Joy and I both feel that it would be entirely inappropriate for him to return here. This may seem hard, but I've put it to him and he accepts it. He remains on his salary for the moment, and I shall, of course, do my best to help him find a job elsewhere.'

Poor bugger, thought Tom. *Woman and*

117

son dead, and now no job.

'How did you feel about him, Dr Crowe? Did you like Harry Benedict?'

'Yes, I did as a matter of fact. Despite the bad feeling he caused, he did have genuine flair. I'll miss him.'

'One last thing,' Tom said. 'I can understand why Benedict came back here on Saturday morning, but what about Kelso? Why did he come to the lab?'

'I can think of no reason other than that put forward by the police: to destroy the result—the correct result—that he'd pencilled on the path form.'

'So you're quite convinced that Richard Kelso was responsible for Peter's death?'

'I thought I'd already made that abundantly clear.' His face, eyes and voice all held the stillness of dislike.

Yes, thought Tom. *Just like Uncle Bill ...*

10

Joy Manners sat in her office and stared unseeing at the balance sheet in front of her. There was a knock on the door and she jumped.

'Yes?'

It opened and Graham Horfield came in.

'Oh, it's you, Graham—what can I do for you?'

'Could you put this through, please, Joy?'

She took the sheet of paper from him and scanned it. 'Isn't this the stuff Harry was ordering last week?'

'Yes. Dr—'

'Oh, for God's *sake!*' She slapped it down on the desk. 'You're supposed to be short of staff—how can you be thinking of doing this now?'

Graham said quietly, 'I'm sorry, Joy, but Dr Crowe asked me to.'

Joy shut her eyes, compressed her lips a moment. 'No, Graham, I'm sorry. We're all on edge at the moment. Leave it with me and I'll have a word with him, OK?'

'OK.' Graham turned to go, but there was another knock; the door opened before Joy could say anything and this time it was Dr Crowe.

'Joy—' he said. 'Oh, hello, Graham.'

'I was just going, Dr Crowe,' Graham said.

Crowe stood to one side to let him pass, then ushered Tom in. 'Joy, this is Mr Jones, the man from the Department of Health. He wants to talk to you about the recent tragedy. Mr Jones, Joy Manners, my laboratory manager.'

Joy came from behind her desk. 'Hello.'

119

Her handshake was firm, although her palms were slightly damp. She was in her late thirties, Tom thought, and her face was attractive, even pretty in a cherubic sort of way, but he could see that the body beneath the sensible skirt and jumper was teetering on the slide into shapelessness. Her office was smaller than Crowe's, more cluttered.

Crowe said, 'My understanding was, as you know, Joy, that Mr Jones's brief was to address any shortcomings in the computer system.' He paused. 'It now seems he's been asked to go further than that and to exclude the possibility of a culprit other than Richard.'

Joy quickly glanced at Tom, then back at Crowe.

'I'm sure he'll explain it to you.' Crowe said.

'Of course I will.' said Tom, trying to hide his irritation.

'Good. I'll leave you to it, then.' The door had begun closing behind him when it opened again. 'Oh, Mr Jones, I'd appreciate it if you'd come and see me tomorrow and give me an update. Shall we say ten again?'

'All right,' said Tom, after a pause. 'Ten—barring unforeseen circumstances.'

'Good. Until tomorrow, then.' This time, the door completed its journey.

'Er—have a seat, Mr Jones.' Joy indicated a chair in front of her desk, then sat down herself. 'So how can I help you?'

Funny how people say that, thought Tom, as he explained the Trust's position to her, *when it's so often the last thing they want to do* ... 'So I am looking for flaws in the computer system, as Dr Crowe said, but I do also have to try and find out exactly what happened.'

'I see,' she said, cautiously.

He opened his notebook. 'Dr Crowe was telling me that you actually had to break up a fight between Kelso and Benedict last Friday. Perhaps you could start by telling me about that, please?'

'Yes ... Well, the two of them had disliked, *loathed* each other for some time. I think it might be easier if I went back a bit, Mr Jones.'

Tom thought quickly; after Crowe's evasiveness, he was determined to pin down a few facts in this interview, especially since Crowe had 'fingered' Joy as one of Benedict's enemies. 'For the moment, I'd just like to know about the fight, if you don't mind, Miss Manners.'

'Very well.' She gathered her thoughts and described how she'd stopped the fight and disciplined Harry and Richard.

'So Kelso was quite badly hurt?' Tom said.

'Oh, definitely—he was in agony, doubled over.'

'Did you apportion blame?'

She hesitated. 'I was in a difficult position—they were both in the wrong, and yet I knew that Richard had been sorely provoked. You see—'

'Even though it was he who'd struck the first blow?'

'He was *provoked!*' She took a breath, continued in a quieter tone: 'Besides, the blow didn't strike, it missed. Harry was much the stronger of the two and he knew it, and his behaviour earlier in the day—'

'I'd like to move on to the evening now, if you wouldn't mind,' Tom said.

Her mouth trembled slightly. Tom continued: 'We know that the change in the computer which led to Peter's death was made at 5.36—you were here in the building at that time, I believe?'

'I left just before then, at 5.35.'

'But you had seen Richard Kelso shortly before that?'

She told him how she'd found Richard in his lab working on Peter's test—no, he hadn't been alone, Amina was there as well, and no, she hadn't seen him working on the computer. 'He was still working on the test itself when I left him. I decided not to wait and went home.'

'At 5.35?'

'Yes.'

'How did you know it was 5.35?'

'I looked at my watch.'

'Did anybody see you leave?'

'Yes, Amina had gone downstairs by then and was in the hall. I asked her to tell Richard I'd had to go and then went home.'

'So you had no further contact with Richard that day?'

'I had no further contact with Richard ever.'

'No,' Tom said. Everything so far accorded with her statement, maybe it was time to open it up a bit. 'I'd like to go back to the fight now. Did you discover exactly what caused it?'

She said quietly, 'I was trying to explain that to you earlier, Mr Jones.'

Tom smiled at her. 'I'm sorry if I seem abrupt, Miss Manners—I have to fix events in my mind before looking at what lies behind them.' He paused. 'You told me earlier you heard Harry accuse Richard of wanting Amina for himself.' As he said this, he realised that he was thinking of them now by their Christian names, as though he knew them better. 'Was there any truth in that?'

'Of course not,' she said scornfully.

'They were just friends. To make any sense of it, I'll have to go back a little—*if* that's all right with you?'

Tom gave her a nod.

'Good.' She seemed to have regained her poise, he noticed. She told him how Harry and Amina had started an affair a few months after he'd arrived. 'This worried me at the time. You may think it none of my business, but Amina was from a strict Muslim family, and her father was in the process of arranging a marriage for her. She'd never even had a boyfriend before, let alone someone like Harry.'

'How do you mean, someone like Harry?'

'To put it bluntly, Mr Jones, he's woman mad, a satyr.' She swallowed. 'Anyway, when her father found out, he disowned her, threw her out, and I had to arrange hospital accommodation for her.' Her eyes slanted away. 'I had tried to talk to her about it, to warn her, but she wouldn't take any notice of me.

'Anyway,' she repeated, looking back at Tom, 'a couple of months later, Harry and Tania—that was Richard's fiancée—suddenly announced that they were going to live together.'

'Just like that?'

'Yes, just like that—they put a notice up on the board. I was shocked myself,

124

so goodness only knows what Amina and Richard must have felt like.' She smiled wryly. 'Well, I do have some idea. Amina locked herself in her room and I was afraid she was going to do something stupid. And Richard ... well, Richard was frankly murderous, and I don't use the word lightly.'

'What had their relationship been like before?' Tom asked. 'Richard and Harry's?'

'Neutral. They were colleagues, nothing more.'

'It can't have been very easy for you, managing the laboratory afterwards.'

It had been hell, she said, they'd refused to speak or communicate with each other and it had made for a terrible atmosphere. 'I was hoping that Harry and Tania would leave—I even suggested to Harry that they should.'

'How did that go down?'

'He told me to—er—MYOB.'

Tom smiled. 'What had your relationship been like with Harry before that?'

'Not particularly good.'

Tom didn't say anything to this and she continued, 'Harry Benedict is a clever, but an essentially destructive person. What Richard did was appalling and inexcusable, but to my mind, Harry brought it on himself.'

Tom wondered for a moment whether

to follow this new strand, then decided to leave it till later.

'What about Richard at this time?' he asked. 'You used the word murderous just now—in what way was he murderous?'

On the day it had happened, she told him, he'd gone into Harry's lab and shouted at him, threatened him. She'd made him take the rest of the day off and had then spent the evening with him. Afterwards, he'd become very withdrawn, *morbidly* withdrawn.

'Didn't this improve with time?'

'Yes, it did, gradually, but things kept happening to inflame his hatred. First, Tania became pregnant almost straight away, then—'

'Why should that particularly inflame his hatred?'

'Richard had always wanted children—he was the paternal type, much more so than Harry. Then, six months after Peter was born, Tania was killed—in a crash that was almost certainly Harry's fault.'

'You'd think a tragedy like that would have made them bury their differences.'

'Oh, not at all. Richard was much worse afterwards. He kept saying that Harry had killed her.'

'What about Harry himself?'

'He had a month off, which was fair enough—he was badly shocked as well as grief stricken. But it was what he did when he came back that really pushed Richard to the edge.' She paused, a dramatic pause.

'What did he do?' Tom asked to fill it.

'He took up with Amina again.' She sighed, theatrically. 'This time, I really did give her a talking-to, but she was beyond reasoning. She said that it was right for her to comfort Harry in his hour of need—pure self-delusion.'

'Did you talk to Harry about it?'

'Just the once.'

'MYOB?'

'Exactly. By this time, it was becoming very difficult to feel sorry for him any more.'

'So your relationship with him was as bad as ever?'

'Yes.' Another sigh. 'Have you ever noticed how after a tragedy, people—even those who dislike each other—really do make an effort to get on? You think: *Perhaps it's a new beginning* ... but it never is.'

Tom nodded sympathetically. 'And you find that the old enmities, when they do return, are often even worse than ever.'

'You're so right! You know, I really tried to build bridges with Harry ...' A look of wariness came over her and she tailed off.

Tom tried to keep the flow going: 'You

said just now that Harry taking up with Amina again pushed Richard to the edge ... why should that have been?'

'I'd have thought that obvious enough —Tania not dead two months and Harry carrying on with another woman right under his nose? His grief went deep! And what's more, with a member of Richard's staff, someone he liked—and I do mean *just* liked—a vulnerable girl who would be hurt.'

'Was she hurt?'

''Course she was—Harry dumped her after a couple of months for an inflatable doll of a nursing sister.'

'But they'd never actually come to blows before, had they? Not until last Friday. I still can't understand exactly what sparked that off.'

She explained about the syphilis project and what Richard had told her of Harry's initial reluctance to involve Amina. 'He's *very* possessive about that project, I can tell you. Anyway, later in the canteen, he apparently changed his mind and told Amina she could be involved after all. Richard was watching them and said that Harry was deliberately leading her on, teasing her, just to spite him—Richard, that is.'

'That sounds a bit Machiavellian.'

'Yes,' she leaned forward, 'but doesn't it

tell you something about Richard's state of mind?'

Tom didn't reply and Joy continued, 'Anyway, then Harry's girlfriend—I won't tell you what Richard called her—made her entrance and Amina exited in tears. Richard followed and spent the next half-hour trying to comfort her, then they met Harry at the lab entrance ... and the rest you know.'

Do I hell! 'But to actually *fight* with him, in public—nothing like that had ever happened before, had it? There *must* have been some other reason.'

'No, it was an accumulation of things, the final straw.'

'Surely Amina knew that Harry had this girlfriend?'

'You're right, of course, but that's the effect Harry Benedict has on people.'

'What d'you mean by *people?*'

'I mean women,' she said. 'Some women.'

'All right.' He paused. 'I'd like to go back now to something you said earlier—you said that *what Richard did* was an appalling thing. Does that mean you're convinced that Richard did do it? Deliberately and maliciously altered that result?'

'I am, Mr Jones, yes,' she said, looking straight back at him. 'It gives me no pleasure to say it, because, despite everything, I liked Richard.' She paused. 'You know, it has occurred to me that he didn't think Peter would die, that he only wanted to give Harry a shock.'

'But he must have known it was at least a strong possibility.'

She shrugged helplessly. 'Who can tell, given the state he was in?'

'You also said that although it was an appalling thing, Harry Benedict had, in effect, brought it upon himself. Isn't that rather hard? I mean, *he* doesn't seem to have had much luck in all this, does he?'

'I suppose it might seem that way to an outsider.'

Tom put on a pained expression and Joy said, 'Have you ever had to work with someone who's truly destructive, Mr Jones? It's no joke, I can tell you. This laboratory was a happy place until Harry Benedict came here.'

'Oh come, Miss Manners. Isn't that just possibly golden retrospect?'

'No, it is not!' she snapped. '*I* could see what he was like when we interviewed him, but Dr Crowe wouldn't listen to me—of course, *he* didn't have to work with him, *he* wasn't the one whose authority was being constantly undermined—'

She broke off, looked at Tom with her head slightly to one side. 'I suppose that was intentional?' Well, my dislike for

Harry Benedict's no secret. But it took a special kind of hatred to want to harm his son, and that's what Richard had by this time—a special kind of hatred.'

11

Tom looked back at her impassively, let the silence hang.

She said, 'I can see now what Dr Crowe meant—we do seem to be a long way from computers.'

He smiled, opened his case and brought out the computer printouts. 'I expect you've seen these before.' He laid them in front of her. 'This is the result put in by Richard at 5.35, and this is what he apparently changed it to a minute later. Does anything strike you about them?'

She glanced at them briefly. 'Only that whoever did it knew exactly what he was doing.'

'Why d'you say that?'

'Because only the Gentamicin has been changed. Whoever it was knew that Gentamicin would be used.'

'Dr Crowe told me that anyone who knew any microbiology would know that.'

'Yes, but the one who'd realise it most

quickly would be the person who'd just read the test.'

'That person being Richard?'

'Exactly.'

Tom frowned thoughtfully. 'So he'd have logged on to the computer and—' he looked up— 'what was his password?'

'BITCH,' she said, then: 'I found that out during Mr Parker's investigation.'

'You didn't know it beforehand.'

She shook her head. 'No.'

'Could anyone else here have known it?'

'I doubt it. I know people do sometimes get to know each other's passwords, but I don't think so in this case.'

'Why not?'

'Because Richard was the type who'd keep it to himself.'

Mm ... 'You told me earlier that when you went to find Richard, he was having difficulty with the test. Can you explain why, in idiot's terms?'

'Surely, but it would be much easier if I showed you.' She started to get to her feet.

'All right,' said Tom, not moving, 'but there were a couple of other things I wanted to ask you first ...'

—No, she could think of no reason why Richard had come back to the lab the next morning, other than what the police had suggested; and yes, she supposed he could use her room to interview Amina. 'Although I'd appreciate it if you didn't take too long,' she added.

'I'll try not to.'

'Good. Shall we go to Richard's lab—' She stopped short. 'I must learn to stop calling it that ... the *main* lab, I'll take you to the main lab.'

She pulled on a white coat and found a spare for Tom. The main lab was at the opposite end of the corridor from Harry's and about half a dozen people were working at their benches. They worked in silence; the only sound was the roaring of Bunsen burners. The stink from the specimens made Tom recoil.

'Simon,' Joy called out to Richard's deputy, totally oblivious to it, 'd'you know where Amina is?'

'Over in the library—she should be back by one.'

'Can I borrow one of these?' She selected a path form from the basket on his desk, then took some transparent plastic plates out of the fridge. Beckoning Tom, she took them to a bench in a corner, sat down and turned on an anglepoise lamp.

'What we do in this laboratory—what Richard was doing last Friday—is to try and grow the bacteria from an infected site, so that we can identify them and find out what antibiotics they're sensitive to.' She was on home ground now and her voice, although quiet, was confident and assured.

She showed Tom the path form. 'This man has been operated on, successfully, for abdominal cancer, but the wound's become infected. It could keep him in hospital for weeks, it might even develop into septicaemia, so they've taken a swab from it and sent it to us.'

Tom could see the man's name, James Macloud: a real name, a real person with real suffering, unlike Joseph Bloggs ...

'D'you know what these are?' She indicated the plastic dishes.

'Plates for growing bacteria?'

'That's right, and this jelly-like substance in them—' she picked one up to show him— 'is blood agar.'

Tom, who'd forgotten his queasiness until the miasma hit him, saw the familiar colour and felt the all too familiar dizziness ripple over his forehead and down his back ... *It's when it catches me unawares*, he thought, gripping the sides of his seat. 'Why blood?' he made himself ask.

'Because a lot of bacteria like it, and because it helps us to identify them.' She hadn't noticed anything.

She indicated what looked like a splash of clotted cream clinging to the bright red agar. 'The swab was inoculated—rubbed —here, and the plate was then incubated overnight. Each of these little dots is a colony of bacteria that's grown up from a single organism.' She held the plate under the lamp to show him. 'This particular organism is *Staph. aureus.*'

'The same type that killed Peter Benedict?'

'Yes,' she said shortly.

Once they'd identified the organism, she explained, they put up an antibiotic screen, by spreading some of the organism over another plate and adding paper discs containing antibiotics. 'The next day, this is what we get.' She picked up another plate; the bacteria had grown, covering the agar in a creamy crust, except in the areas surrounding some of the discs.

'The bugs won't grow around the antibiotics they don't like; this one here, for instance.' She pointed. 'Ampicillin. There's no growth, which means the organism's sensitive to it. That's what they'll probably treat him with.'

'And that's the sort of test Richard was trying to read?' Tom said.

It was, she agreed, but the plate Richard had been trying to read had been incubating only seven hours, the borderline of readability. 'Not only that,' she continued, 'but it was also a Direct

Sensitivity. That means that the original swab itself was inoculated directly on to the plate and the antibiotic discs added. We do that for an urgent case, because it gives us a result a day early. D'you follow me?'

'I think so, yes.'

Direct Sensitivities were tricky things at the best of times, she told him, and after only seven hours, it wasn't surprising that Richard was having difficulties. 'The irony is that if he *had* made a genuine mistake, no one would have blamed him.'

'Harry Benedict might,' Tom pointed out.

'No one taking a dispassionate view, then.'

'Did you see the original plate yourself?'

'Yes, when the police called me in on Saturday.'

'Did it agree with the first computer result?'

'Perfectly.'

'So Richard had, in fact, successfully read this tricky and difficult test?'

'Yes.'

'And then pencilled the results, *correctly* on to the form; entered them, *correctly,* into the computer; and then had a brainstorm and changed one of them?'

Joy sighed. 'I know it doesn't sound so likely when you put it like that, but you didn't see him that day. Or the weeks and months beforehand. Richard was over the edge.'

Tom looked round. 'Which terminal was he using?'

'That one.' She pointed.

'How did you know, if you didn't see him using it?'

She shrugged. 'It's the nearest.'

'All right. How many terminals are there in the building?'

'Oh, let's see ... three in here, two in Harry's lab, I've got one, Dr Crowe's got one ... there's another in the lab office and two more downstairs.'

'Could you show me, please?'

'Surely.' She switched off the lamp and put the plates away and Tom felt better as soon as they left the room.

The lab office was next to Harry's lab. 'Was there anyone in here when you left?' he asked.

'Not so far as I know.'

She showed him the reception offices downstairs and their terminals, also the tea room next to them.

'Are these locked when the staff go home?' Tom asked.

'No, only the main entrance.'

He stood silently for a few moments, looking round.

'Have you finished with me yet, Mr

Jones?' she asked him, rather pointedly.

'I think so. Oh, there was one other thing ...' He asked her why Richard had insisted on telling the ward sister alone that Peter's result was in the computer. 'It did strike me as carrying security a tad too far.'

Joy smiled grimly. 'Maybe it did, but then you haven't had to put up with the mistakes caused by phoned messages. The wards are demanding them more and more, and they take up a great deal of our time. And as if that wasn't enough, they scribble them down on scraps of paper, lose them, and then have the gall to accuse *us* of—' As though aware that she was losing control again, she stopped herself. 'That's why we instituted the system,' she finished lamely.

'But wouldn't a house officer or staff nurse do? I mean, it does put a lot on the sister, doesn't it?'

'In practice, we do usually tell a doctor or staff nurse, but Richard used to insist on going by the rules.'

'Why was that?'

'Partly because it was his lab that caught most of the flak ...' She hesitated. 'But also, I suspect, because he didn't like this particular sister.'

'Oh? Why was that?'

'Because she's the inflatable doll I was

telling you about—Harry Benedict's latest conquest.'

'I see,' said Tom slowly, thinking: *It doesn't sound as though you like her much either ...*

She said, 'I'll tell Amina you want to see her when she comes back, shall I?'

'If you would, please.' Tom glanced at his watch. He not only wanted to see Amina, but if possible, before Joy had a chance of speaking to her. 'Miss Manners, I was hoping you wouldn't mind showing me the canteen ...'

Joy's expression indicated that she minded quite a lot, so he added mendaciously, 'Dr Crowe suggested I ask you.'

'I'm sorry,' she said firmly, 'but I'm afraid I can't at the—' She caught sight of Graham through the hatch and called him over. 'Are you going to the canteen, Graham?'

He was.

'Oh, good—perhaps you'd like to take Mr Jones with you?'

Sure, Graham said. He didn't have a great deal of choice and neither did Tom. 'This way,' he said, and Tom followed him.

They walked in silence for a few moments, following the covered walkway Harry had taken the previous Friday. The bright sunlight picked out the grass forcing its way through the cracks in the paving, and the rust streaking the curved corrugated iron sides of the passageway in front of them.

'Quite a contrast in building styles,' Tom said. 'I suppose all this'll be knocked down before long?'

'I dunno that it will,' Graham said. He had a closed, slightly foxy face and an accent like that of the topers in the Fleet. 'The Yanks built it to last, and as long as it stays up, I can't see the Trust spending any money they don't have to. Besides,' he added with a grin as he held one of the rubber flaps open, 'this bit's Grade Two listed.'

'You're kidding.'

'Just down here ...'

In the alcoves either side of the canteen entrance were two of the most ornate displays of wood carving Tom had ever seen. The first depicted monks dispensing food and medicine in a monastery, the other, doctors and nurses ministering to patients in a hospital ward.

'Who did these?' Tom asked.

'Italian prisoners of war.'

'Yes, the colours are a bit exotic for Brits ...' The shapes and figures were lovingly coloured, reds, golds and blues predominating. 'Are they really Grade Two listed?'

'Sure.'

Tom admired them for a few moments more, then Graham opened the door for him and they were surrounded by the chatter-clatter and smells of the canteen.

Tom bought Graham's meal for him and they sat down. Graham said suddenly, 'Is it true you're down here to look into Peter Benedict's death?'

'That's right. Why d'you ask?'

'Harry Benedict's my boss.'

Was, Tom thought, *was your boss.*

'Can I speak to you in confidence?'

'Of course you can.'

He leaned forward. 'I don't know what you've been told about Harry, though I can guess some of it, but ... well, I just wanted to say that he's always been OK to me. He's OK to anyone so long as they don't mess him about.'

'How long's he been your boss?'

'Since he came here, about two and a half years ago.'

'Did you ever work with Richard?'

'Yeah. He was all right too, though not so much fun.'

'In what way?'

Graham thought about it while he took a mouthful of food. 'Richard was good at his job, but Harry finds ways of making the work interesting. For instance ...' He told Tom about the syphilis project and how

141

Harry had involved him in it. 'He's the real drive behind it,' he finished. 'Without him, it would never have even got started.'

'I suppose you can understand Richard hating him the way he did, though,' Tom said after a pause.

'Yeah, that's Harry's problem—women.'

'Thinks with his balls, you mean?'

Graham grinned. 'I don't think *thinking* comes into it much. The thing people forget, though,' he continued, 'Harry likes chatting up the girls—he can't help it—but it's them that make the running.'

'How d'you mean?'

'Put it this way.' Graham lowered his voice. 'It was Tania that chased Harry, not the other way round. He just couldn't resist what was on offer.'

'What about Amina, did she chase him?'

'Well, not exactly, but she made it pretty plain she was available.'

Tom would have liked to have heard more, but by now it was nearly one and he was still hoping he might find a way of intercepting Amina, so he made his excuses and they went back.

He found Joy's office door open. Inside, a willowy, blonde girl stood staring out of the window. She turned as he came in.

'Oh! Hello.'

'Hello,' Tom said. 'You don't know where Miss Manners is, do you?'

142

'No, I was looking for her myself.' She appraised him briefly—her eyes were a striking green, he noticed. She said, 'Are you the man from the Department of Health who's come about the—the tragedy?'

'Yes,' Tom said cautiously.

She took a step towards him. 'I'm Teresa Belling. Tania Belling was my sister ... Harry's Tania. Peter was my nephew.'

12

Amina threw down her pen with enough force to make some of the others in the library look up, gathered her books and walked out.

'Joy's been asking for you,' Simon told her when she got back to the lab.

'It's all right, I know about it. I'll see her later.'

He looked at her. 'Are you all right?'

'Just tired.' She tried to smile. 'Didn't sleep much last night, that's all.'

'You're on call tonight, aren't you? D'you want me to do it?'

For a moment, she was tempted ... no, she needed the money. 'Thanks, Simon, but I'll be all right.'

Simon left and she sat and gazed out of the window, wondering what she could do ...

It had been Simon who'd told her the evening before, just as they were all going home, that Dr Crowe wanted to see her.

'What's it about?' she'd asked.

'I don't know. Joy's with him.'

Normally, this would have been the cue for much ribaldry: *What you been up to then, Amina? It'll be fifty lashes this time ...* and so on, but since the deaths they'd all gone about their work in silence, speaking only when necessary.

She'd hung up her coat and started along the corridor. She'd been torn by indecision since Peter's death: to send condolences or not to send them? In the end, she'd done nothing. She knocked on Crowe's door.

'Come ... Ah, Amina—come and join us.'

She sat next to Joy, and Crowe told her about Tom's impending visit. 'Since the two of you were with Richard at the time, he'll be wanting to speak to you,' he said.

She'd walked out of the lab and over to the cycle shed ... *Not more questions, I can't bear it ...* unlocked her bike and wheeled it out before mounting and starting for home.

The cycle track ran from the hospital to within half a mile of her house and, as she pedalled along it, the breeze and the evening sun brought the poplars that lined it to shimmering life; soft air stroked her face and despite everything, she felt her mood lift a little. At its end, the track merged with a side street running downhill to one of the main roads out of town.

It wasn't until she was half-way down and the slipstream was lifting her hair that she gently braked to cut her speed—only to find that the brakes had no effect. She yanked them on as hard as she could—nothing ...

She was going quite fast now and could see the traffic streaming past on the road ahead. Her eyes hunted around for another side street, although she already knew there wasn't one. She was about to jump off and risk the broken bones when she spied a garden hedge on the other side and, without thinking, veered across the road in front of a car, narrowly missing a woman with a pram before ploughing into it.

She felt the shock as the hedge embraced her, although she felt no pain and heard only silence in the seconds that followed, then there were sounds: a car door slamming, running feet—then hands gently pulled her out and a voice said 'Are you all right?'

Someone said, 'I think so …' then she realised it was herself.

A woman said, 'Stupid cow, she nearly hit my baby.'

More voices: 'Shall I phone for an ambulance?'

'No, I think she's only shocked.'

Only shocked …?

But it was true, she'd ducked her head as she'd struck, so her face wasn't even scratched.

'She nearly hit my baby.'

'What happened, love?' the car driver asked.

'I—I don't know … the brakes didn't work …'

'I'm not surprised.' Someone else had pulled her bike out and was trying them. 'Look at this—they've been slackened off so the blocks don't touch the wheels.'

'Did you do that, love?'

'No, of course not.'

'Then I'd say someone's got it in for you.'

There was a silence. She looked round. She could make out individual faces now: the car driver, the cycle expert, the woman with the pram.

'And she nearly hit my baby,' the latter repeated, but when no one took any notice, flounced off in high dudgeon.

'D'you want me to take you to the police

station?' the car driver asked.

'No, it's all right,' Amina said. 'Thank you. It's just an accident. Please, I'm all right, I just want to go home now.'

'I think you should go to the police,' the bike expert said.

'All right, I will,' Amina said. 'After I've been home and changed.'

The car driver had put her bike into his boot and driven her home, but she hadn't gone to the police. She hadn't been able to sleep, either ...

'Amina?' She jumped back to the present and looked round to see Joy.

'Your nephew?' Tom said.

'Yes,' Teresa said. 'Could I speak to you about it—in private?'

There were footsteps in the corridor outside. Tom found his wallet, whipped out a card and gave it to her. 'I'm staying at the Regency Hotel.'

She slid the card into a pocket, then her eyes flicked over his shoulder.

'Teresa, what are you doing here?' Joy asked.

'I did say I was coming to see you, Joy.'

'Yes, but ...' She turned quickly to Tom and hastily introduced him to her companion. 'Mr Jones, this is Amina Khatoon—I'll leave the two of you,

147

OK? Teresa, if you'd like to come with me ...'

Teresa followed her out and the door clicked firmly shut.

She couldn't get her out of here fast enough. Why?

Tom gathered his thoughts and turned back to Amina.

'Miss Khatoon, do sit down.' He proffered her a chair, then took the other and placed it so that they were facing each other. 'I'm Tom Jones from the Department of Health.' *Holly was right, she is pretty, but why so nervy ...?* Then he remembered that Joy would have probably warned her about him.

'It's Amina, isn't it? Well, Amina, I've been sent here to look into Peter Benedict's death, and since you were involved, I need to ask you some questions.' He decided not to tell her about Holly yet.

'All right,' she said.

'I'd like to start with last Friday, the day Peter died. According to the computer records, you did some preliminary work on his sample?'

'That's right, yes.'

'Were you aware at the time that it was from your colleague's son?'

'Oh yes. I saw the name and asked the others. They told me that Peter had been admitted.'

148

'Could you describe what you did? In layman's terms.'

She'd made a film from the swab, she told him, Gram stained it and examined it under the microscope. Then she'd entered her findings into the computer and phoned the ward ... Her voice was low, musical, the slight singsong quality making it the more attractive, Tom thought.

'What were your findings?' he asked.

'A lot of pus cells, which indicates an infection, and also Gram positive cocci in clumps, which is suggestive of *Staph. aureus.*'

'Did you do anything else?'

'Yes. I cultured the swab and made a Direct Sensitivity plate—that's a test—'

'Joy's explained that to me. Did you tell Harry Benedict what you'd done?'

'Er—yes. I went to see him about something else an hour or so later and told him then.'

What was it she'd gone to see him about? he asked, and she told him about her Master's degree, how in the canteen Harry had changed his mind about involving her in the project, and, as she spoke, Tom could see a delicate flush diffusing into her skin.

He said, 'From what I understand, his girlfriend then came in, you left and Richard Kelso followed you?'

'Yes.' She swallowed, looked away.

Tom said carefully, 'I'm aware that you and Harry had a relationship in the past. Was it because of that that you left?'

'Yes. I know it sounds silly now, but it did upset me at the time.'

'It doesn't sound silly at all,' he said gently. 'So you left and Richard followed. What happened then?'

'He took me to his car and we talked.' She hesitated. 'I know I had no right to be upset ... it was just the way she took over, brushed me aside as though I wasn't there ... but I *was* upset and Richard listened to me, he was a good friend.' *Why am I telling him this?* she wondered, her eyes pricking.

Tom pulled a tissue from the pack on Joy's desk and handed it to her. 'I'm sorry if you find it distressing.'

'No, it's all right.' She blew her nose. 'Please go on with your questions.'

'What I really want to know about is Richard's mood, his state of mind at this time.'

'Well, he was extremely irritated with me for even asking Harry in the first place—he had warned me not to—but mostly, he was very angry with Harry. We talked for, I don't know, half an hour, then we—'

'What did you talk about?'

'Oh, things.'

150

'What things?'

After a pause, she said, 'Oh, just how I felt about Harry.' She quickly went on to tell him how they'd met Harry outside the lab and she'd gone to fetch Joy. Tom knew she was hiding something, but decided to let it go for the moment.

'You were with Richard later, I believe, when he was in the main lab examining Peter's Direct Sensitivity test?'

'Yes. He was going to give me a lift home.'

'And Joy came in?'

'Yes.'

'What was Richard doing at that moment. With the test?'

'He was trying to read it.' She gave a faint smile. 'He was irritated at her interruption, I remember, and told her, rather pointedly, that he would see her later.'

'And she left?'

'Yes. And I left just afterwards to give him some peace to read the test.'

'What was he actually doing as you left the room?'

'He was studying the plate with his lens.'

'Did you see him working on the computer?'

'No.' She shook her head.

'What time did you leave the room?'

'A little after half-past five, I suppose.'

'Presumably, his next step would have been to write the results on the form, and then put them in the computer?'

'Yes, presumably,' she agreed.

'What was his password?'

'It was—er—BITCH. One of the others told me. It was fairly general knowledge.'

So much for password security ... 'So you left Richard alone. What did you do then?'

'I went downstairs and waited for him in the tea room.'

'You went there straight away?' Tom asked.

'Yes.'

'Joy told me she found you in the hall when she came down.'

'That was just after I got down. I went to the tea room after that.'

He studied her face, but it was still flushed from his previous questions. 'Did Joy say anything to you?'

'Only to tell Richard she'd had to go.'

'What time was that?'

'I'd guess about twenty-five to six.'

Hmm ... 'How long after that did Richard come down?'

'Five, ten minutes.'

'Did he say anything when he came down?'

'He called my name, asked if I was ready.'

152

'So he had to look for you?'

'Only in the tea room, then he drove me home.'

Had he said anything to her on the way?

—Only to ask how she was feeling. He'd been very withdrawn.

Had she invited him in?

—Yes, but he'd refused.

Could she think of any reason why he'd returned to the lab in the morning?

—Only what the police had suggested —to destroy the path form he'd written on.

Hmm again ... 'OK. I'd like to go back now, Amina, to when Harry first came to work here. That was about two and a half years ago, wasn't it?'

She blinked. 'Yes.'

'How long after he came did you form a relationship with him?'

'About three months.'

'How long did the relationship last?'

'Oh, about four months.' She looked directly back at him. 'Mr Jones, I know you had to ask me about last Friday, but I don't understand the relevance of my past relationship with Harry.'

'I'll explain. You told me just now how angry Richard was at the way Harry treated you in the canteen, angry enough for him to physically attack Harry. If I'm to be persuaded that Richard Kelso did the thing everyone says he did, I have to understand *why*. That means building up a comprehensive picture of the relationship between them.'

She gave an irritated shrug. 'Oh, very well.'

'What was the relationship like between them at that time? When you and Harry were going out together?'

'It was neither one thing nor the other ...' She hesitated. 'Although Richard didn't *like* Harry even then—he did warn me to be careful of him.'

'Careful in what way?'

'Not to trust him, not to let my family find out about him.'

'But they did find out, didn't they?'

'Yes, because I told them,' she said defiantly. 'I knew my father was arranging a marriage for me and I thought it was my ... my duty to let him know.'

'Your duty?'

'Yes.' She went on to tell him how she'd been disowned and Joy had found her hospital accommodation.

'Why didn't you move in with Harry?' Tom asked. 'I mean, it was because of him you had to leave home, wasn't it?'

'I ... because he didn't want me to. He said we weren't ready yet.' She swallowed again. 'I should have known then.'

'How long after that was it that Harry left you for Tania?'

'I ... a month, six weeks ...'

'It must have been a terrible shock for you.'

Her eyes became trance-like, her voice somehow juvenile. 'He told me a week earlier that he needed ... more space, that he needed to think about our relationship ... then, on that Friday morning, he told me ...' She tailed off.

'What did—?'

'He told me how sorry he was ... I believe he really meant it ...'

After a pause, Tom said, 'What did you do then?'

'Oh, I went to my room, locked the door and cried. Joy came over, but I told her I wanted to be alone.' She tried to smile. 'You know, like Greta Garbo. I think she thought I was going to kill myself.'

'Did you feel like killing yourself?'

She drew in a breath. 'I may have toyed with the idea, but it would never have come to that.'

I wonder ... 'Do you remember how Richard took it?'

'I didn't see him for several days but when I did, well, you couldn't help notice how angry he was. He'd always been so calm, and then suddenly, he was murderous.'

155

That word again. 'Did he speak to you at all about it? I mean, you had both been ... *betrayed.*'

'Not then, no. He was very withdrawn. It was Joy who helped me most.' She didn't react to the word he'd used.

'It didn't occur to you to leave?'

'I had no home, Mr Jones, no family. This place was the only security I had.'

'What about Richard, didn't his mood improve with time?'

'He did seem to recover, a little, but he was never the same person. He was very quiet, very bitter.'

'I wonder why *he* didn't leave.'

'I suppose he had nowhere else to go either.'

'And then Peter was born?'

'Yes. Richard was very upset about that, I remember.'

'Why? I mean, they were living together, so why should having a baby make it any different?'

'Because it set a seal on things, I suppose,' she said slowly.

'How did *you* feel about it?'

She shrugged. 'Neither one way nor the other. As you said, they were living together.'

'But then, Tania was killed.'

'That was when Richard became very peculiar,' she said, looking up at him. 'He

156

blamed Harry, of course.'

'And you went back to Harry, didn't you?'

'Yes.' She gave a twist of the lips. 'Richard was very angry with me—it was the first time he'd ever been really angry with me.'

'Why *did* you go back to Harry?'

'Why does anybody do anything, Mr Jones? Because I loved him, I suppose.'

'Do you still love him?'

She stared past him, silent, motionless. 'Yes,' she said at last, her mouth hardly moving.

'How long did it last this time?'

'Two months.' Her voice was completely toneless.

'Did you live with him this time?'

'No.'

Tom knew he wasn't going to get any more, it was as though the final admission had drained her—and the phrase about dabbling in the stuff of people's souls rose accusingly in his mind.

'How did it end?'

'He just told me,' she said tonelessly. 'He was embarrassed, ashamed—'

So I should bloody think ...

'—he said he wasn't ready for the commitment I wanted.'

'One last question, Amina. You knew Richard as well as anyone, you were

157

with him just before and just after this thing was done—do you really think that Richard Kelso did it? Deliberately killed Peter Benedict?'

She looked back at him. 'Oh yes, he must have. Something just snapped that day under the strain. It wasn't premeditated or anything. Perhaps he didn't even realise what he was doing at the time. I don't know. But he did it, Mr Jones, I'm quite certain of that.'

After she'd gone, Tom tapped a thoughtful fingernail on the desk for a moment, then flipped through his notebook, trying to compare events as she'd related them with her statement, and with what Joy had told him.

It was no good, he'd have to draw up a flow chart to do it properly, perhaps this afternoon back at the hotel ...

He found himself massaging his temples —yes, back to the hotel, where he could take some more painkillers for his head, although perhaps he'd better arrange something with Harry Benedict first.

There was a tap on the door, which then opened.

'Seems funny, knocking on my own door,' said Joy. 'Have you finished yet, Mr Jones?'

158

'Very nearly, Miss Manners. A couple more minutes?'

'All right.'

'And one phone call,' he added with a smile.

'Long distance?'

'No, local. In fact, you could help me—d'you have Harry Benedict's number?'

'Oh, yes.' She came in, opened a drawer and took out a small, stiff-covered book. 'In there, under B.'

She went out, pulling the door closed behind her again. Tom found the number and dialled. He was about to give up when it was answered.

'Yeah, hello.'

'Is that Harry Benedict?'

'Who is this?'

'I'm not a reporter or anything like that. My name's Jones and I'm from the Department of Health.'

'Oh?'

'I've been sent down to look into the computer aspects of your son's death. I'm sorry to intrude on you at this time, but it would be a great help to me if I could speak to you ... Mr Benedict ... ?'

'Yeah, I'm still here.' There was another silence. 'When did you have in mind?'

'Sometime this afternoon, if possible.'

There was a pause, then, 'What about in an hour—hour and a half?'

'If that's all right with you, yes.'
'D'you know where I live?'
'Yes.'
'I'll see you then, then.'

Tom replaced the receiver and went to tell Joy she could have her room back.

13

She'd tried everything she knew to arouse him, to make him forget for a few minutes, but nothing had worked.

'It doesn't matter, Harry,' she said at last.

He was staring up at the ceiling. 'No.'

Sally saw that he meant it, that for the moment he was beyond her reach, but she was saved from having to say anything by the summons of the telephone below.

'Better answer it,' she said. 'It might be important.'

He grunted and rolled out of bed.

'Was it?' she asked when he came back. 'Anything important?'

'Some guy from the Department of Health.' He slid back beneath the duvet. 'Wants to talk to me about the computer aspects of Peter's death, for God's sake! He's coming here in an hour.'

160

'D'you want me to go?'

'No.' His face suddenly crumpled and she took him in her arms.

'Let it come out, Harry ...'

But he couldn't even cry properly; somehow, he was beyond her reach even for that.

The door, which could have done with a coat of paint, opened to reveal a man a couple of inches taller than Tom, but with a similar whipcord body and London hungry face.

'Mr Benedict?'

'Mr Jones? Come in.'

He closed the door behind Tom, then led the way off the hall into the living-room. A stunningly attractive girl was sitting on the sofa.

'This is my girlfriend, Sally,' Harry said.

'Hello,' said Tom, his thoughts irresistibly drawn to the film *When Harry Met Sally*.

This Sally got to her feet and said with a dazzling smile, 'It's hello and goodbye, I'm afraid. I'm just going.'

'Not because of me, I hope.'

'No, I was going anyway. I'm on duty in an hour.'

'Oh yes, you're the sister on the Children's Ward, aren't you?'

161

'Yes?' Her tone made it a query.

Tom said, 'Mr Benedict probably told you why I'm here. I'd like to come and speak to you sometime if I could, please?'

'All right,' she said. 'When would suit you?'

'Tomorrow morning?'

'I shan't be on duty again until tomorrow evening. Could you come this evening?'

Tom groaned inwardly; the paracetamol he'd taken hadn't done much for his head and he felt completely spent. 'What time this evening?'

'Just after six?'

That wasn't too bad, although he might miss dinner—again. 'OK.'

'It's Children's Ward A.' She told him how to find it, then smiled at him again as she made her exit.

While Harry saw her out, Tom looked around the room. It had the feel of having been put together by a woman although the general untidiness suggested some time ago.

Harry came back in. 'Sit down, Mr Jones. D'you want a coffee?'

'I wouldn't mind. Thanks.'

'Milk and sugar?'

'Just milk, please.'

He sat down on the sofa as Harry went out again. It was still warm from where Sally had been sitting. What on earth did she see in him? What did *any* of them see in him?

He was London all right, from his thin, creased face to his thin flat accent, from the north-east, Tom thought, Walthamstow, for choice—He stopped, reminding himself that this was a man who'd lost not only his son, but also his son's mother, and he wondered what had made him forget. Was it what Amina had told him? Or Sally's presence, perhaps?

He looked round the room again for a picture of Peter or Tania, but couldn't see one. There was a goodish music centre, large TV, not many books—although the watercolour over the mantelpiece looked like an original, low coffee table with overflowing ashtray ...

Harry came back in, bearing two mugs.

'Milk, no sugar, right?' He seemed tidy enough: clean jeans and denim jacket, clean hair, although the lines in his face ran deep and the skin around his eyes was baggy and bruised.

'Thanks.' Tom took the proffered mug. 'You're from the Department of Health, you said?'

'Yes.' Tom had been wondering what approach to use with him and still hadn't made up his mind. 'And I'm sorry to be intruding at this time.'

'So you said on the phone.' Harry's lips

briefly compressed in something between a grimace and a smile. 'Thanks, anyway.'

It was somehow a weak mouth, Tom thought, at odds with the rest of his face. He explained how the Trust wanted to make sure the computer couldn't be abused in such a way again, then decided to plunge.

'The first thing I need to be certain about is whether it really was Richard Kelso who changed that result.'

Harry stared at him. 'Of course it was Richard Kelso.'

Tom said, 'I can appreciate your feelings about him, Mr Benedict, but I hope you can appreciate my need to be objective. Why are you so sure it was him?'

'Haven't the police told you?'

'They have, yes, but I'd like to hear it from you.'

Harry said, 'Well, for a start, he as good as admitted it.'

Tom stared at him. 'He *admitted* it?'

'As good as.' He took a cigarette from the pack in his breast pocket and lit it. 'D'you want one?'

'No, thanks. When—?'

Harry said, 'You wouldn't believe I'd got it down to ten a day, would you? Now look at me.'

Tom said, 'When did he as good as admit it to you?'

164

'When I found him in the lab. Look, he didn't actually say he'd done it, it was what he did.'

'What did he do?'

'It was written all over his face when he went for me—'

'Wait a minute, please,' Tom interrupted. 'This was on the Saturday, the morning you ... killed him?'

'Yes.'

'Could you tell me what happened before that?' He dragged out his notebook. 'That morning.'

'Yeah ...' Harry drew heavily on the cigarette, ash fell and scattered, and the tip glowed. 'Well ...' He swallowed, looked down at the carpet. 'I woke up feeling pretty terrible, had some coffee, then I remembered Tania's parents—Tania was Peter's mother. They hadn't been told yet, so I rang them.'

'What time would this have been?'

'About eight.' He smiled mirthlessly. 'Her sister offered to come round—'

Did she now?

'—but I told her I didn't want to see anyone. Anyway, after that, I got to thinking about how it didn't make any sense, Peter dying like that. The more I thought about it, the less sense it made, so I drove to the lab to look at the plates.'

'How long was this after you'd phoned Tania's parents?'

Harry shrugged. 'I dunno—twenty-five minutes? Anyway, when I got there, the first thing I saw was Richard's car, parked outside the door. I went in. It was dim and I couldn't see properly at first, then I saw him on the stairs. He was staring at me with this *caught in the act* look on his face. He yelled something at me, *you bastard*, I think, then he went for me. We fell, he got hold of my hair and was bashing my head on the floor ...'

'You say he had a *caught in the act* look on his face—can you describe it?'

'Well, his face sort of collapsed when he saw it was me, his mouth fell open ... then he was on me. I can't say any more than that.'

'So he didn't actually *say* anything, other than *you bastard?*'

'He didn't have to.'

Tom thought for a moment. 'Joy Manners told me you were stronger than him—how come you couldn't just overpower him?'

'He was strong enough then—he came at me like a windmill in a force 10. I suppose fear must have given him the strength. I didn't mean to kill him, I was just trying to hold him off. Anyway, I've been all over this with the police—'

'What happened next?'

'I tried reviving him and when that didn't work, I phoned for the ambulance and police. Then ... well, I *had* to find out about Peter's tests, so I went upstairs and looked. I found the path form, which had written on it that the bug was resistant to Gentamicin. Well, you'll know if you've been talking to the others that he was treated with Gentamicin, because Richard had said it was sensitive. Then I found the plate, and there it was, *resistant* ... then I turned on the computer and it said bloody *sensitive.*'

'Did you realise at that stage it had been changed in the computer?'

'Not then, no ...' He was staring at the cigarette in his fingers; the smoke was rising in a zigzag from where they were trembling—he quickly stubbed it out. 'Anyway, then I heard the police arriving and went back downstairs.' He looked up at Tom. 'D'you really want to know all this? I thought your interest was in the computer.'

'I'm interested in exactly what happened with the computer, and who it happened with. You say it was Richard—I want to know everything about him.' He paused. 'I'd especially like to know why he came back to the lab that morning.'

'The police say it was to get rid of the

path form he'd written on.'

'If that was the case,' Tom said slowly, 'he must have arrived only just before you.'

'How d'you mean?'

'You said in your statement that you didn't know how long he'd been there when you arrived. Well, he must have only just got there, or he'd have already destroyed the path form.'

'I suppose that's right,' Harry said slowly. 'Anyway, whatever the reason was, he went for me as soon as he saw me. If you've spoken to the others at the lab, you must know how things were between us.'

'Well, he certainly seems to have had his reasons for disliking you. But then again, so have some of the others.'

'Maybe they have, but not as much as him. Besides, *he* was the one doing the test, putting in the results, phoning the ward.'

Tom leaned forward. 'So why did he put the true result in first? Why didn't he put the false result in straight away and pretend it was a mistake?'

He shrugged again. 'I suppose because it didn't occur to him at first.'

'Joy Manners and Amina Khatoon were also in the lab at that time. Neither of them has much reason to like you—why couldn't it have been one of them?'

'Because there simply wouldn't have

been time for them to do it.'

'There might, actually.' Tom told him about the possible two-minute gap between the two results.

Harry's face went very still as he thought it out. 'That's pretty wild,' he said at last. 'No, I don't believe it ... it has to be Richard.'

'But why? As I said, both Amina and Joy have good reasons for disliking you, especially Amina.'

Harry lit another cigarette. 'I know that I've treated Amina badly. I didn't want to, it just happened that way.' He blew smoke. 'But she wouldn't do a thing like that.'

'What about Joy, then?'

'More likely than Amina, I'll grant you, but I still can't see it.'

'Why more likely than Amina?'

'Because she's spiteful, and because she *thinks* I treated her badly.'

'Why should she think it if it wasn't true?'

Harry leaned forward. 'Because she's incompetent, and incompetent people always blame others for their own shortcomings.'

'Dr Crowe doesn't think she's incompetent. Neither did I, for that matter.'

'She's OK with bread and butter and figures, but she's *scientifically* incompetent, and that's where she insists on prodding her nose in.'

Tom was aware that his questioning had taken on an urgent, almost adversarial quality; he also knew that he shouldn't allow his growing dislike to affect it, but every instinct told him that Harry was holding something back and he wanted to tease it out.

'You said just now that you treated Amina badly. Having spoken to the others in the lab, I'd agree with you. You not only treated her badly, but did so consistently, over a period of time. Right up to the last Friday, in fact. Why are you so sure that she wouldn't have done it?'

Harry looked at him a few moments before replying. 'Because she just wouldn't. Strange though it may seem, she loves me.'

'Love can turn to hate, especially under the kind of pressure you've applied.'

'I *know* Amina. *Dammit!*' he shouted suddenly. 'It's because of her that *Richard* did it ... ! Sorry ...'

'Oh yes, the fight between you and Richard.' Tom's voice remained calm and smooth. 'That was because you flirted with her in the canteen, wasn't it? Led her on. Why did you do that?'

Harry made a visible effort to control himself. 'She'd asked me if she could be involved in a project I'm working on, and I was telling her she could. I was doing her a favour.'

'That's not how Richard saw it.'

'Well, he wouldn't, would he? That's what I'm trying to tell you—everything I did was wrong in Richard's eyes.'

'Knowing that, knowing Richard was there and knowing your girlfriend was about to come in, it wasn't—'

'I *didn't* know my girlfriend was coming in! She'd only told me a few minutes earlier she couldn't.'

'All right, but knowing how Amina felt about you, it still wasn't a very clever thing to do, was it?'

Harry's eyes slid away. 'Maybe not.'

Tom had a flash of insight. 'You *did* do it deliberately to goad him, didn't you?'

Another pause. 'I suppose I did. In part, anyway.'

'For God's sake, why?'

'Because I felt like it,' Harry said with a rush of bravado.

Tom stared at him. 'Here's a man who's volatile and hates you, a girl who's crazy about you and he's fond of ... you must have had more reason than that.'

'I suppose I did.' It came out sullenly.

'What was it?'

Harry lit another cigarette from the stub of the old and, haltingly, told Tom about his row with Joy over the project, about Crowe then telling him he must include

171

her in it, and his realisation that Richard was behind it.

'I was sick up to here of his sniping at me and when I saw him glaring at me in the canteen, I went and sat with Amina.' He let out a sigh. 'I *did* do it to annoy him, but then I had the idea that involving Amina might help me keep Joy out of it, as well as doing Amina a favour. I do feel badly about her, as it happens,' he added.

Tom shook his head in amazement. 'I can't believe you lot.' He paused. 'It doesn't sound to me as though Dr Crowe's got a lot of time for you either.'

'Oh, that's just him keeping the plebs in their place.'

Tom said, 'Your strategy of goading Richard certainly worked, didn't it?'

'It wouldn't have, not like that, if Sally hadn't come in when she did.'

'Although when you think about it,' Tom continued, 'Amina can't have been very happy either, can she? You didn't just upset her, you *humiliated* her.'

'I didn't intend to. But the fact is, she then went and sobbed on Richard's shoulder, and he was the one who went for me.'

'The fight, you mean?'

'Yes.'

'I've been wondering about that ... if he was prepared to fight you, knowing he wasn't as strong as you, would he have then done something so underhand as to try and harm your son?'

'I hurt him in that fight. I did it to bring it to an end, but it did hurt him.'

Tom kept silent, and after a moment, Harry continued, 'You've probably heard the history. Tania was engaged to him before she moved in with me, then she was killed and he blamed me for it. And then I—I hurt Amina, more than once, as you said. Then on Friday, I goaded him into attacking me, and then thumped him in the gut.' He leaned forward again, held Tom's gaze. 'So later, when the opportunity suddenly arose, he took his revenge.'

'But he must have known he'd be found out.'

'Only if it was discovered he'd changed the result, otherwise it would have just looked like human error.'

'Would you have accepted that?'

'Probably not, but everyone else would.'

'All right. One more thing—I believe you were over in the Children's Ward when Richard phoned to tell them the result was in the computer?'

'Yes, I was in with Peter.'

'Were you aware that Richard was waiting on the phone to give Sister the message?'

His eyes flickered. 'I was aware that *someone* was,' he said. 'I'd gone out to the duty room to find out what the hell was going on, chase the lab if necessary. The student nurse, the one with the missing link, told me the lab had phoned and that she was going to go and find Sally.'

'What time was that?'

'I wouldn't know exactly—sometime after 5.30.'

'When did Sister come back?'

'I don't know that either. At the time I was just relieved the lab had got round to producing a result at last.'

'So you don't have any idea of how long Richard was waiting on the phone?'

'No, none—although Sally did tell me later about what he'd said. I can't think it was all that long.'

'So why did Richard make such a point of it?'

Harry said wearily, 'I've no idea.'

14

Back at the hotel, Tom rang Chris Parker and arranged to see him first thing in the morning, then phoned Marcus.

'Tom—how's it going?'

'All right.'

'It doesn't sound like it.'

'I've got a filthy headache I can't shift.'

'Self-inflicted?'

'No, overwork.' He told him how he'd met Liz the previous evening and what they'd worked out between them.

'But there still wouldn't have been enough time for anyone to alter the result, surely?' Marcus said.

'There might. I've had an idea and I'm seeing the computer chief again tomorrow about it. And two of the lab staff do have pretty strong motives, as well as opportunity.' He gave him a run-down of the day's interviews.

'Well, they're certainly worth following up,' Marcus said. 'What did you make of Benedict?'

'Just about the most selfish and graceless individual I've ever met.' He described Harry and some of his peccadilloes. 'I can't for the life of me understand what all these women see in him,' he grumbled.

'Ah, Tom—*If women like them like men like those* ...'

'Yeah, yeah—*Why don't women like me?*' Tom finished. 'That's not what I—'

'And he has suffered a shattering double bereavement,' Marcus continued quietly. 'Grief can bring out the worst in people. *You* ought to know that.'

'Yeah, all right.' Tom knew that his own behaviour hadn't been particularly gracious when Frank had died.

'So what's your next step?'

'I'm just off to talk to the sister in the Children's Ward—the one who also happens to be Benedict's latest girlfriend.'

'That is a rather bizarre coincidence, isn't it?'

'I suppose so, although not so much when you consider the way Benedict puts it about.' He looked at his watch. 'Anyway, Marcus, I'd better go, if I'm not to be late for her.'

He swallowed some more paracetamol and went down to his car. The traffic was still heavy and it was six by the time he'd parked and threaded his way through the flowered courtyards of the New Hospital to the modest, unassuming entrance of the Old. Inside, his eye was caught by a much polished brass plaque attached to the wall and something made him stop for a moment and look at it.

This hospital is respectfully dedicated to the American Doctors, Nurses, Administrators and Technicians who came here in time of war to serve their fellow citizens.

He followed the signs up the wide, old corridors, thinking: *It's a part of our history,*

this place—maybe it is worth preserving ...
A door opened and a porter emerged, pushing an old lady in a wheelchair. Her body was wasted and her face a mosaic, but her eyes missed nothing and she grinned conspiratorially at him.

He found Ward A and pressed the intercom button. A tinny, and somehow irritating, voice answered almost immediately.

'Children's Ward A, Student Nurse Ashfield speaking.'

He told her who he was, and about half a minute later the door was opened by Sally herself.

'Come in, Mr Jones. We'll go to my office.' As she shut the door, he became aware of the indefinable odours of the infirm. 'You had no difficulty in finding us, then?' she asked.

'No.' Trying to distract himself, he watched her as she walked just ahead of him—nurses' uniforms aren't generally designed to flatter, but Sally somehow gave this one a life all of its own.

'In here.' She shut the office door and found him a chair. 'Now, how can I help you?' She sat down herself and carefully crossed her legs. 'I can't imagine that I can, very much.'

'You never know, sister,' he said, smiling at her—she really was very attractive. He

177

briefly explained why he was there ... 'So I'd be grateful if you could tell me about events as you saw them from here.'

She considered a moment. 'Well, the first I knew was when I found Harry at the ward entrance ...' She took him through the day until she'd gone off duty just after six.

'You know the rest of the story,' she finished, looking more sombre than when she'd begun.

'Yes.' Tom looked up from his notebook. 'When did you find out that Peter had died?'

'Not until I came on duty the next day.'

'You hadn't contacted Harry meanwhile?'

'I did phone in a little before eight, but everything seemed to be all right at that stage. After that, I went out—to a concert we'd both planned on going to. I wish I hadn't, now.'

'What concert was that?' he asked, curious.

'The Bournemouth Symphony Orchestra, Mozart and Haydn.' She smiled, sadly. 'I've been trying to introduce Harry to some culture.'

I'd have thought clubland more your scene ... 'Did you try to contact him after you had found out?'

'Yes, I phoned his house the next morning and was very worried when there was no answer, although nothing like so worried as when the inspector arrived and I found out what *had* happened. It was a nightmare, the worst day of my life.'

'You're fond of Harry?'

Her eyes, clear violet eyes, flicked sharply back at him, but before she could say anything, the phone rang.

'Sister Yate, Children's Ward A ... Well, he was asleep when I saw him a few minutes ago, Mrs Underhill ... Yes, he is ... Yes, we'll see you then.' She gently replaced the receiver and turned back to Tom. 'To answer your question Mr Jones—yes, I am fond of Harry, very fond.' She hesitated. 'I know he's not at his best at the moment, but he's a good man who's been devastated by the loss of his son. And apart from anything else, he needs me.'

'Yes,' Tom said. Then: 'There are one or two points I'd like to go over with you, if you wouldn't mind?'

She glanced up at her clock. 'So long as it doesn't take too long.'

'According to Harry, you told him you couldn't go to lunch with him in the canteen that day, and yet a few minutes later, you did manage to join him?'

'That's right. Jane, my staff nurse, came back early from her own lunch.'

'This may seem trivial, but I'd like you to try and remember what you saw when you got to the canteen. Did you know Richard Kelso by sight?'

'No. He's been described to me since, but I can't remember seeing him.' She smiled. 'I do remember the doe-eyed girl who was sitting with Harry.'

'Why do you remember her?'

'Because she quite clearly had a thing about him. I've a feeling I may have upset her—she left shortly after I arrived.'

You know perfectly well you upset her ... 'You didn't see anyone leave with her?'

'No—although I'm aware now that they did.'

'How long did Harry stay with you after that?'

'About half an hour, I think. He waited while I finished my lunch, then we came back. Peter's nanny, Marie Davidson, was here. She was marvellous, a saint. She stayed with him all day until after I'd gone off duty.'

'OK. I'd like to come now to the critical time, 5.30, when everything seemed to happen at once. Dr Miller had asked the lab to read the Direct Sensitivity Test, you were called away, Harry came over to see Peter, and then the lab rang back but refused to speak to anyone except you.'

'I was called to Ward B just *after*

Harry arrived,' Sally said, 'to put in an IV—intravenous—line.' She continued quietly, 'I did wonder at one stage whether it would have made any difference if I hadn't been called away at that moment, but the police say not.'

Tom kept his ideas about that to himself. He said, 'It does seem to be a crazy system, though.'

'Which d'you mean? The system that called me away, or the one whereby the lab wouldn't speak to anyone except me?'

'Well, both, now you come to mention it.'

'The fact that I was called away you can blame directly on the Trust ... only please don't quote me.'

'If I repeated all the things I've been told about Trusts,' Tom said, 'I'd be jailed for inciting civil unrest.'

She smiled, then said, 'It's a simple cost-cutting exercise. They've done away, on some wards, with the requirement to have a sister present at all times. Well, that's fine until a situation comes along that must have a sister to deal with it, such as putting in an IV line. For that reason, a lot of us here are on call to other wards, and, as you can imagine, the call always comes at the worst possible time.'

'It's called Murphy's Law.'

'I always thought it was called Sod's Law.'

Tom looked up—the vulgarity seemed somehow incongruous in her precise accent—then he smiled inwardly as he remembered the earthiness of some of the other cut-glass nurses he'd met. 'What about the other system?' he asked, 'The lab only giving messages to a sister—even so simple a message as: *The results are in the computer.*'

'Well, to tell you the truth, Mr Jones, I think there's an element of spite there.'

'On whose part?'

'The microbiology lab's. We've had arguments with them for years about phoned messages. They always say they've phoned them and that we've lost the message, when we know damned well they've forgotten to phone. We were forced into the system, oh, about a year ago, and it's been a real pain. We were hoping that the arrival of the computer would be the end of it—we never dreamed they'd insist on keeping it.'

'But they did?'

'Yes, they did. But what was doubly unfortunate on this occasion was that the phone was answered by our student nurse, Katie Ashfield, who's frankly a complete dork, and then that the person on the other end apparently insisted on speaking to me. They're not always quite so dogmatic as that.'

'This student nurse, she's the one who went looking for you?'

'That's right, but somehow managed to miss me. I came back and saw the phone lying on the desk, picked it up and found myself being roundly abused for having kept him waiting so long.'

'Can you remember exactly what he said?'

She thought. 'He asked if it was Sister and I said it was, then he said: *At last—Peter Benedict's microbiology results are in the computer.* I thanked him, then he said: *Do you realise how long I've been waiting here?* I said: *Well, don't blame me for that,* and hung up on him. It was his tone as much as what he'd said.'

'Do you have any idea of how long he'd been waiting?'

'Obviously not, but Nurse Ashfield told me later that she couldn't have been away more than a minute or so.'

'Is she here at the moment? Nurse Ashfield?'

'Yes.'

'I think I ought to see her while I'm here.'

Sally hesitated. 'All right, but please bear in mind what I told you and go easy with her.'

'What is the problem with her?' Tom asked.

She sighed. 'She was wished on us by another ward. I accepted her as an extra, but she's turned out to be one of those extras that are a minus rather than a plus.'

'In what way?'

'Her attitude, mostly. She should never have been accepted for nursing training, but they're reluctant to get rid of them once they've been taken on.' She paused. 'Shall I get her for you now?'

'Could I have a look at the room Peter was in first?'

'There's another patient in it at the moment, but you can see it from the outside, if you like.'

'Please.'

She stood up and he followed her round the corner to the duty room.

'That's it—Number Three,' she said, pointing.

Outside the brightly painted glass door, a staff nurse was in deep discussion with a good-looking young doctor.

'And that's the nurses' station, where I took the call,' Sally said. Tom lowered his voice. 'And is that, er ... ?' He nodded in the direction of the nurse working at the station.

'Nurse Ashfield, yes. D'you want to use my office to speak to her?'

'If you wouldn't mind.'

Sally called her over and explained what Tom wanted.

'All right,' she said.

He took her back to the office, sat her down, smiled encouragingly and said, 'Katie, I'd like you to think about last Friday, the day Peter Benedict was admitted.'

'Yes.'

'Were you in the duty room when Dr Miller asked the lab to read the Sensitivity Test?'

'Yes, I remember that.' She had a flat Midlands accent, slightly adenoidal.

'And then Sister Yate was called away?'

'Yes, that was just after Mr Benedict arrived.'

'What happened after that?'

'Mr Benedict went in with his son and Dr Miller went off somewhere. Then the lab rang.' Her face was rather like her voice, he thought: flat, inexpressive, unemotional.

'This is the important bit—can you remember what the person in the lab said? As near as possible.'

'He asked for Sister, I told him she wasn't here and said I'd get Staff Nurse, who was in Number Six. He said ...' She frowned as she thought about it. 'He said: *You know the rules, Nurse, it has to be Sister.*

Then he said: *Just go and get her, will you, this is urgent.* He was very abrupt about it, quite rude.' Her cheeks flushed slightly as she remembered.

'And there was no one else around you could ask to take the message?'

'I didn't know where Dr Miller was—besides, I don't think he'd have spoken to him.'

'So you went straight to look for Sister Yate?'

'Yes. Well, almost. Mr Benedict came out, wanting to know whether we'd heard from the lab. He was rather rude as well—but that was because he was worried about his son,' she added hastily.

'So, then you went to Ward B to look for Sister?'

'Yes. They told me I'd just missed her, and when I came back, she was speaking to him on the phone.'

'How long would you have said you were away?'

'Not very long—a minute or so.'

'You're sure about that?'

'Yes.'

Tom let out a breath. 'Well, that's been very helpful. Thanks, Katie.'

He went back to the duty room with her and thanked Sally. 'One last thing, sister—could you tell me where Ward B is?'

'I'll show you.'

'You don't have to if you're busy.'

'It's no problem.'

In the corridor, she said, 'D'you think you'll get to the bottom of it?'

'I don't know. What I can do, hopefully, is to make some recommendations to ensure it can't happen again.'

They reached the door and he pulled it open.

'Just down there, right, and right again.' She grinned at him. 'Or you could take the scenic route if you wanted—up there, left and left again.'

'Thanks,' he said. 'I think I'll go direct.'

He found the entrance of Ward B, which had a security door like that of A, and thoughtfully looked back. Yes ... if Sally was still on the phone to Richard when Katie got back, then Richard would have been waiting for two minutes at least ...

15

Steam rose in thick layers from the bath, misting the mirror, drifting through the open door, slowly taking with it the headache that had clung to him all day like a parasite.

Bloody Goliath ... he thought.

He'd interviewed five people—six, if you counted Graham—taken nearly twenty pages of notes and nothing, *nothing* was going to shift him—

The phone rang.

Oh, kiss off ...

But the years of conditioning were too much and he heaved himself out and dripped his way over to it.

'Hello.'

'Mr Jones?' A woman's voice.

'Speaking.'

'It's Teresa Belling here. We met today in the microbiology lab.'

'Oh, yes, Miss Belling.'

'Have I caught you at a bad time or something?'

'I was in the bath.'

'Ooh, I'm sorry. I was trying to get you earlier and ... well, I need to see you. It's important.'

'Tomorrow sometime?'

'I was hoping you could spare me a few minutes now ... I'm in the hotel bar.'

'What, this one?'

'Yes. I was going to leave a message if you weren't in.'

'All right,' he said resignedly. 'Give me quarter of an hour.'

He tried snatching a few more minutes in the hot water, but the magic was gone and after a moment, he hauled himself out again and reached for the towel.

Most of the customers in the hotel bar had little more character than the bar itself, so he was able to pick her out quite easily, sitting on one of the plush seats that lined the wall. She sat up and gave him a wave.

'Thanks for seeing me,' she said as he reached her. 'Sorry about your bath.' She was wearing a cream-coloured woollen dress that emphasised the slenderness of her figure.

'What can I get you to drink?' Tom asked.

'Oh no, let me ...'

He smiled. 'Do you have an expense account?'

'No.'

'Well, then.'

'Aqua Libre then, please.'

One of the new health freak generation, he thought as he made his way over to the bar—not that he wanted any alcohol himself that night. He ordered two Aqua Libres and took them back over.

'Thank you.'

'How can I help you?' He grinned inwardly as he heard himself using the inane phrase, took out his cheroots and lit one—and intercepted a disapproving

189

glance. *Tough,* he thought. *She dragged me out of my bath.*

She said, 'Joy told me that you've been sent here to confirm that Richard Kelso killed ... killed my nephew.' She looked suddenly stricken and Tom realised that she was younger than he'd thought at first, not yet twenty.

'Joy had no right telling you that,' he said quietly.

'What are you here for, then?'

Covering Mrs Castleton's bum ... 'Primarily, to make sure that the computer system can't be abused in such a way again.'

'So you *do* think it was Richard.' It came out as an accusation. 'Well, that's what I came here to tell you—it couldn't have been.'

'Why not?' he said after a pause.

She looked at him for a moment, then said, 'Richard Kelso loved my sister body and soul. He could have no more harmed her child than he could have harmed her.'

'Love—that kind of love—can do strange things to a person—' Tom began.

'Oh, don't patronise me.'

'I'm not patronising you. What I'm saying is that, according to his colleagues, your sister treated Richard very badly, and under those circumstances, love can turn into hate.'

'But Richard wasn't *like* that.' She shook her head slightly, as though puzzled that he couldn't understand.

'I'm sure he wasn't originally, but from what everyone says, he did become that way.'

'He wouldn't have killed Peter.'

Tom said, 'He had several shocks ... blows, over a period of time. Your sister breaking off their engagement, Peter's birth, then your sister being killed. And since then, a perpetual state of guerilla war with Harry.'

'No ... I mean, yes—he hated Harry and would have harmed him if he could, but not Peter.'

'But Harry *was* harmed, in just about the worst way possible.'

'Not by harming Peter, he wouldn't.'

'We're going round in circles.' Tom said. He looked at her. 'Is there something you haven't told me?'

She drew a breath. 'I came to know Richard very well while they were engaged. He was a bit slow and old-fashioned, but I—I liked him, because he was so *straight*. I *know* that he couldn't have done it.'

Tom regarded her in silence.

She said, 'All I'm asking is that you think about it ... look at other possibilities.'

'That's exactly what I have been doing,'

he said with a smile.

'That's all right then.' She picked up her glass, drained it and banged it back on the table. 'That's all I wanted to say. Thanks for the drink, Mr Jones.' She started to get up.

Tom put his hand on her arm. 'Wait a minute, please.'

She looked down at his hand; he removed it and she sat down again.

'I *am* looking at all the possibilities, and I will bear in mind what you've told me.'

'OK. That's good.' She hadn't forgiven him.

He was sure there was more, but sensed that pressurising her wouldn't help. 'Perhaps you could help me ...' *Softly* ... 'Were you surprised when your sister went to live with Harry?'

'Gobsmacked. I told her what a fool she was, but she was too far gone.'

'Did it work? The relationship?'

She hesitated. 'They squabbled quite a lot, but it was that sort of relationship. I think it was Peter that held it together.'

'Would it have lasted?'

'I don't know,' she said after a pause. 'And I can't see the point of these questions.'

'They help me to get an idea of the whole picture. Did you like Harry?'

She screwed up her nose. 'Not really.'

'You disliked him?'

'No, not that either.'

'Strange,' Tom mused. 'Everyone else I've spoken to either loves him or hates him.'

'Oh, that's 'cos he's dripping with sex appeal.'

'It's not the sort of thing I'd notice,' Tom said drily. 'His sex appeal didn't do much for you, then?'

'No, because he's weak. That's why his life's such a mess, because he's basically a weak person.'

Which is about the most perceptive observation I've heard about him yet ... 'Did you see much of Richard after the engagement was broken off?'

'Yes, a few times, and I know what you're thinking. Yes, he was bitter, who wouldn't be?' She leaned forward. 'But he *still* didn't kill Peter.'

'Did you go and see Peter much?'

'While Tania was alive, yes. Not so much afterwards. I regret that now. My parents used to go and see him.'

'I can't imagine they liked Harry very much.'

'Not much, no.'

'Was Harry a good father?'

'Ye-es ... Although he used a nanny a lot after Tania was killed, Marie something.'

'With a full-time job, he didn't have much choice.'

'I suppose not.'

Tom searched his tired mind for a way to keep the conversation going, 'What did Tania look like?' he asked. 'Were you and she alike?'

'Not really. I've got a photo of her somewhere.' She prodded about in her bag, handed him a snapshot. 'I took it the day after she moved in with him.'

It was at a disco or club of some sort—strobe hazed an upper corner. Tania was in the middle, laughing, radiating joy. She had one arm around Harry, who was grinning broadly, the other round a younger man. You could see that she and Teresa were sisters, but Tania was fuller in face and body—older, more mature, less beautiful, sexier.

He handed it back. 'There was quite an age gap between you.'

'Yes, six years.' Teresa suddenly looked sad again. 'We'd really only just got to know each other.'

By now, Tom's headache had evolved into a scarlet pulse behind his eyes and he couldn't see which way to go.

'You're very certain about Richard, aren't you?'

She nodded. 'Yes.'

'I need more than just your certainty.'

'Can't you just accept that I *know?*'

'If you really do know, there must be something you haven't told me.'

'I've told you all I can,' she said quickly, 'and now, I really must go.' She got to her feet. 'Thanks for the drink.'

Damn! He shouldn't have pushed it. 'Where can I contact you?'

She hesitated. 'I'm staying with my parents at the moment.' She gave him the address and hurried away.

Back in his room, Tom took some more paracetamol and went to bed. But not to sleep.

Despite the loopholes he'd found, he'd been coming round to the probability of Richard's guilt, but now ... She nagged at him, Teresa, nagged at his headache. For all her naïvety, there was something convincing about her, and that had to be because she hadn't told him everything.

Amina was asleep when the phone beside her bed rang about three hours later. She pushed herself up, wondering where she was for a moment, then switched on the bedside light and picked up the phone.

'Hello?' she said sleepily, then: 'I'm sorry, could you speak up, please?'

'Is that the on-call microbiologist?'

'That's right, yes.'

'This is Dr Ware on Ward Five. We've got a query meningitis and I'm sending some CSF over.'

'Er—can I have the patient's name, please?'

'Poole. Like the town.'

'Have you taken the sample yet?'

'Yes, it's on its way to you now.'

'I'll go straight over.'

She quickly dressed in jeans and sweat shirt, found her keys and the personal alarm and let herself out.

The on-call bedrooms had been built near the pathology labs, but the micro-biology lab was about seventy yards away. Amina hated every one of those yards.

She took a breath and walked quickly, trying to avoid the shadows. It was chilly and a slight mist haloed the lamps. A couple of minutes later, she let herself into the lab.

Moonlight filtered into the hall, lighting the marble stairs but making the shadows around them seem tangible, almost threatening, until she found the light switch.

That's better, she thought. She wasn't superstitious, but it still wasn't very pleasant to be in the dark by herself in the place where Richard had been killed so recently.

She looked in the tube reception box, but the sample hadn't arrived yet, so she

196

went upstairs to turn the equipment on. That done, she went back down to check the box again.

Nothing. She waited a few more moments, then went back upstairs to phone Ward Five.

The bacteria causing meningitis can usually be identified by Gram film, enabling the right treatment to be started straight away; thus, there's usually no delay in getting a sample of cerebrospinal fluid to the lab.

'Can I speak to Dr Ware, please?'

'We don't have a Dr Ware on this ward ...'

Nor did they have a patient called Poole, nor any patient with query meningitis.

Did I dream it? she wondered. It had happened to some of the others, but never to her before. Had Dr Ware phoned from one of the neighbouring hospitals and neglected to mention the fact?

She tried the switchboard, but they didn't know anything, then three of the nearby hospitals, who didn't know anything either.

She waited another five minutes, then switched everything off and went downstairs.

I'll be just falling asleep when the phone goes again, she thought as she pulled the door to.

A half-moon rode high in the sky and the sound of her footfalls echoed gently from the walls of the New Hospital.

''Night, miss.'

She gave a tiny shriek as a figure emerged from the shadows. It was Len Kozer, one of the night porters.

'Sorry, miss, didn't mean to startle you.'

'It's all right,' she said. 'Good-night.' *Stop being so stupid,* she told herself. Len always made her feel nervous, perhaps because he moved so silently and seemed to be everywhere at once.

An owl hooted, a tawny, she thought, and the sound made her feel slightly better. As she turned into the courtyard leading to her room, the intoxicating smell of night-scented stock filled her nostrils, and as she turned her head to locate the source, she sensed a shadow detach itself from the wall behind her—

She tried to duck as something swung at her head, then she was on the ground and the shadow was systematically kicking her about the chest and belly. She instinctively curled into a ball, tried to scream, but nothing came.

The kicking stopped; she sensed acute danger—rolled over as something solid struck the ground beside her ... She rolled again, thrust her hand into her pocket, found the alarm and pressed it as something crashed into her head ...

Her eyes opened, focused on the face of Len Kozer, and this time she did manage to scream.

16

By nine the next morning, when Tom passed through, the sun had burned away the mist and the little courtyard overflowed with light and warmth. Flowers cascaded from concrete tubs and there were even a few bees buzzing round them, although closer inspection revealed these to be drones, expelled from the hives now that their usefulness was over.

Don't get too excited, boys, mused Tom, who'd woken clear of head and eye and was on his way to see Chris Parker. *Indian summer's a con and winter's just round the corner.*

Parker was waiting in his office for him. 'You're not going to tell me you've got doubts,' he said.

'Possibly.'

'There's a politician's answer if ever I heard one.'

Tom told him about the non-existent password security and Parker exploded.

'Oh, I don't *believe* it—it's what passwords are *for*, to prevent this kind of thing.'

Then Tom told him how Joy and Amina had been alone with terminals at the time Richard was entering the results. 'Could either of them have used Kelso's password to get into the system while Kelso himself was still using it?'

'Yes,' Parker said. He added defensively, 'People do sometimes need to go into the system on one terminal when they're already logged on with another.'

'It's OK, it makes sense,' Tom assured him. 'But in that case, could either of them have called up the Results program that Kelso was using, watched while he put the results in, and then altered one of them?'

'No.'

'Why not?'

'Because two people can't access the same patient at the same time. The same program, yes—the same patient, no.'

'But it would have been the same password,' said Tom, 'and therefore, ostensibly, the same person.'

'Different terminal, though. I'll show you if you like.'

'It's all right,' Tom said, 'I'll take your word for it.' He continued slowly: 'So they'd have to wait until Kelso had finished, and since they couldn't know when that would be, they wouldn't have had enough time ...'

'Exactly. On the other hand,' Parker said, 'let me try something a minute ...' He sat down at the computer and quickly resurrected Joseph Bloggs.

'Imagine I'm Kelso, working at his terminal,' he said.

Using Richard's password, he called up the Results program and keyed in the antibiotic results. Then, leaving them on the screen, he went over to the other terminal.

'Now, I'm A N Other.' He logged on, again with Richard's password. 'I can get into the program OK, but if I try to access the same patient, this is what I get ...'

PATIENT RECORD BEING ACCESSED BY ANOTHER USER.

'Now, Tom, you be Kelso. Press Return to put those results in, and then come out of the program, while I keep trying to access it here.'

Tom did so.

'Look at this,' Parker called excitedly. 'I thought so—the moment you came out, I got in.' The program was now on the other screen.

'Try changing the result,' Tom said urgently.

Parker pressed a few keys, the screen flickered and the new result came up.

GENTAMICIN   S

'About five seconds,' said Parker.

'Blimey,' Tom said. 'I thought a minute was plenty, but I never realised it could be done as fast as that.'

'But it would depend on this person knowing that you could do that,' said Parker. 'Are they particularly adept with the system? Bearing in mind they haven't had it all that long.'

'I honestly don't know. I'll have to find out.'

He was on his way over to see Crowe when a car pulled up beside him and the window buzzed down.

'Good morning, Mr Jones.' It was Liz Kendall.

'Hello, Inspector. What brings you here?'

'I'm going to see Miss Khatoon. She was attacked here in the hospital last night.'

'Bloody hell! Was she hurt?'

'Nothing broken, probably because she managed to set off her alarm. A lot of bruising on her chest and abdomen where she was kicked and a blow to the head. They're keeping her in for observation.'

'Any idea who did it?'

She shook her head. 'No.'

'Is it connected, d'you think?'

'That's what I'm hoping to find out.'

Tom said, 'Would you mind if I came with you?' He gave her what he hoped was a winning smile. 'We are supposed to be in a liaison situation.'

She smiled back. 'All right, but ...' She was on the point of reminding him that it would be she, not he, asking the questions, then decided it wasn't necessary.

He got in. 'Can I use your phone?'

'Go ahead.'

He called the microbiology lab and left a message for Crowe that he'd been unavoidably detained.

'The irony is,' he said as she drove to the car-park, 'I've just found out something that makes Miss Khatoon a plausible suspect.' He told her what he and Parker had discovered.

'Interesting,' she said. Then: 'I'd rather you didn't say anything to her about it at this stage.'

Amina was lying in bed with her eyes closed, trying to rest, when the sister brought Liz and Tom over.

'The police would like another word with you,' she said. 'I've told them they mustn't stay long, so if they outstay their welcome, ring the bell.' She wasn't joking.

Amina cautiously propped herself up. 'Hello, Mr Jones.'

Other than for a swollen lip, which gave her a slightly lopsided appearance, her face was unmarked. Her long, dark hair was tied up and there was a bandage round her head.

'How are you feeling, Amina?' Tom asked.

'Oh, you know,' she said. 'Battered, but relieved it wasn't worse.'

'It's Inspector Kendall who wants to speak to you.' He indicated Liz. 'I only came along to see how you were.'

'Oh,' Amina said. Then, to Liz: 'I have already made a statement.'

'I know,' Liz said with a smile, 'I've got it here. I'd like to go over it with you to see if there's anything else you can remember.' Her voice was gentle, inviting confidences.

'All right. Won't you sit down?'

They sat and Liz led her through her story again. When she'd finished, Liz said, 'So Dr Ware was a man, you think?'

Amina hesitated. 'I did think so at the time, but I'm not so sure now. I was half asleep, so it's difficult to be certain.'

'Are you certain about the name, Dr Ware?'

'Yes.'

'You see, we've checked, and there's no

doctor of that name in the region.'

Amina shrugged—she was sorry, but that was the name.

'All right. Now, Amina, try to think ... you're on your way over to the lab—are you sure you didn't see, or hear, anything unusual? Any detail at all ...?'

—Yes, she was sure.

'And on the way back, you saw only the night porter, Len Kozer?'

'Yes,' Amina said with a wry smile. It had been Len who'd heard the alarm and scared the attacker off.

'Now think, Amina ... You've reached the courtyard, you become aware of this figure—is it slim, or well built?'

—Again she was sorry, but she really couldn't say.

'Did you catch a smell of anything? Deodorant, aftershave? Scent?'

'No, nothing like that. The only smell I remember is the night-scented stock. It'll never seem the same again,' she added sadly.

'No,' Liz said. 'You're sure they didn't say anything? Not a grunt as they kicked you? A sigh, a whisper?'

—No, nothing.

'And dressed in black?'

—In dark clothing, yes ... Hair? No, she hadn't noticed any hair.

Whatever angle Liz tried, it seemed that

she couldn't tell them any more. Liz gave it up and said, 'Amina, please be honest with us—is there anyone you can think of who might have any reason to dislike you?'

'No,' she said quickly. 'There's nothing like that.'

'Are you sure?'

'Yes. And I am feeling rather tired now, so if you wouldn't mind ...'

'All right, Amina.' She turned to Tom. 'Is there anything you can think of?'

'Just one thing, Amina. Last night you thought Dr Ware was a man—what made you change your mind?'

'I'm not sure. The voice seemed somehow faraway ...'

'Muffled?'

'Ye-es ... but I was still half asleep, I'm not even sure now I didn't dream it, so it's not surprising I can't remember ...' Her own voice was becoming a little wild and Liz caught his eye and stood up.

'It's all right, Amina, we'll leave you in peace now.'

Tom stood up too. 'I hope you're feeling better soon, Amina.'

She said, 'Could I have a quick word with you, please, Mr Jones? In private.'

Tom glanced at Liz, sat down again as she withdrew.

Amina's tongue touched her lips. 'Did you go to see Harry yesterday?'

'Yes, I did.'

'How was he?'

'Well, he's obviously under a lot of strain,' Tom said after a pause. 'He looked very tired and he was smoking a lot.'

'I'm sorry to hear that. That he's under strain, I mean.' She paused. 'Was he alone?'

Tom decided on the truth. 'Not when I got there, no—his girlfriend was with him. She left soon after I arrived.'

'I'm glad he has company. It wouldn't be good to be alone at such a time. Will you be seeing him again?'

Tom hadn't been intending to, but now thought quickly and said, 'Probably, yes.'

'Will you please tell him that ... he's in my thoughts?'

'Of course I will.' Sensing she'd said all she wanted to say, he continued, 'Amina, I wonder if I could ask you something?'

'Yes?'

'Well, by all accounts, Harry treated you very badly, and yet you seem so concerned about him ...'

'Isn't there an English saying, Mr Jones: *Love is blind?*'

'Yes, but in your case, it seems bereft of any sensory apparatus.'

'I take it you didn't like Harry very much?'

'I did try to make allowances, but ... not really, no.'

'Stress always brings out the worst in him, he says and does things he regrets later.' She regarded Tom a moment. 'I wonder if it's the dislike of similar personalities ...'

'*What?*' Tom was genuinely shocked.

'Oh, but you are alike in some ways. You both have charm, and kindness, but also a certain amount of ruthlessness. I'm quite sure you're ambitious, Mr Jones, and I suspect you have weaknesses—susceptibility to women, for instance. Like Harry.'

Tom was lost for words.

'He was brought up by his mother, you know, who was an alcoholic,' she said, then continued more slowly. 'I think he's been looking for a substitute for her ever since. Were you insecure as a child, Mr Jones?'

He could only gaze at her.

'I can see that you were,' she said. 'I think I would like to rest now.'

'Yes ...' Determined not to let her off completely, he said, 'Oh, I knew there was something I had to tell you—I believe you know my wife, Holly. She said she met you on a course a couple of years ago.'

For a moment, she looked blank, then

she said, 'Oh, Holly Jones ... she's your wife?'

'That's right.'

'I do remember now that she said her husband worked for the Department of Health. What a coincidence.'

And not altogether a welcome one, Tom thought, looking at her.

Liz was waiting for him at the ward entrance, and together they walked down the main corridor.

'Was it anything relevant?'

'She wanted to know if I was seeing Benedict again, and if so, to tell him he was in her thoughts.' He didn't think Amina's observations on his similarities to Harry had any relevance.

'Strange girl,' Liz mused. 'What d'you make of it—the attack? D'you think it's connected?'

'Have there been any previous attacks in this hospital?'

'A few, recently.'

'Mm. I was about to say that the false Dr Ware suggests she was set up for it ... Come and have a coffee with me,' he said suddenly. 'On the NHS.'

'Aren't you supposed to be seeing Dr Crowe?'

'I'd rather have a coffee with you.'

'I'd rather have tea.'

'All right.'

I don't know about women generally, Tom thought a little later, looking across the table at her, *but I am susceptible to this one* ... Her head was slightly to one side, her lips parted in the faintest of smiles and the adrenaline sang in his blood at the nearness of her.

Having extracted a promise that she'd do nothing about it for the moment, he'd told her about Teresa's domiciliary visit and her conviction that Richard had been innocent.

'It probably doesn't mean anything,' he said. 'But if it did, it would put Joy and Amina in the frame.'

'Which of them would you go for?' she said, her eyes on his face.

'Well, they do both have motive and opportunity.' He told her about his interviews with them the day before. 'Before Teresa came along, I'd more or less made up my mind they were telling the truth. If they weren't, they're Oscar material.'

Liz smiled and said, 'You realise that Joy Manners is one of the leading lights in the Theatre Thespians?'

'No,' Tom said slowly, 'I didn't.'

She leaned forward. 'I really do need to speak to Teresa Belling, Tom.'

'Give me till tomorrow morning. Please.'

'All right.'

It wasn't until he'd reached the micro-biology lab that he realised she'd used his Christian name.

17

In Crowe's office, Indian summer had reverted to type.

'Good of you,' Crowe was saying, 'to go and see Amina. Although the connection with Peter Benedict escapes me for the moment.'

'That's why I went, to try and ascertain whether there is one.' Tom, in the low armchair, was peering up at him, sideways, across the expanse of his desk.

'Oh. And is there?'

'We're still not sure.'

'I must say I find it difficult to see how there could be.'

Tom didn't say anything and, after a moment, Crowe continued, 'How was Amina, in herself?'

'Bruised, but nothing broken.' Tom briefly described her injuries.

'Well, I'm glad it's not serious, anyway. I'll have to try and get over myself.' Crowe leaned back in his chair. 'On the subject of Peter Benedict, you were going to give me a progress report, weren't you?' He smiled with his mouth. 'I hear you've been very busy, seeing all sorts of people.'

'Yes.' *Patronising sod.*

'Have you managed to reach a conclusion yet?'

'Not as such, no, although there will have to be some amendments made to your computer system.'

'What sort of amendments?'

'I think it's probably best if you discussed that with Mr Parker.'

As Crowe made a note on the pad in front of him, Tom continued, 'You're also going to have to do something about your password security.'

Crowe looked up. 'Oh? Why?'

'Because it seems that Richard Kelso's password was general knowledge here. Which gives rise to the possibility that someone other than he altered the result which led to Peter Benedict's death.'

'That's a rather sweeping assumption, isn't it?' Crowe said after a pause.

'Not really.' Tom explained what he and Parker had discovered.

Crowe's eyes never left Tom's face. 'So you're saying that it could, in theory, have been someone who was here in the building at the same time?'

'Yes.'

'Which means Amina, Joy ... or myself. You realise I was here as well that evening, don't you?'

'Yes—you told me so yourself, yesterday.'

'So I did.' He leaned back in his chair and smiled, catlike. 'So which of us, I wonder, is your preferred candidate?'

'Amina and Joy do both have motives,' Tom said calmly, determined not to be outfaced.

'If dislike can be counted as motive.'

'I think it's a bit stronger than dislike, Dr Crowe.'

'Let me get this right, Mr Jones.' His tone now became openly scathing. 'You're suggesting that one of them, sorry, of *us*, happened to know Richard's password and also about this quirk in the computer system; happened to be on hand and to know exactly what Richard was doing and when he was doing it, and also just happened to *dislike* Harry enough to want to ... I find the whole idea tenuous beyond belief.'

'But nevertheless possible, Dr Crowe.'

'But the *evidence* against Richard, evidence gathered by the *police*—it's overwhelming. What you're suggesting is ... esoteric.'

'The evidence against Richard is certainly

strong,' agreed Tom. 'But it's circumstantial and falls short of proof.'

'Speaking of proof, I'd be interested to hear how you'd go about proving your theory.'

'That I can't say for the moment.'

There was a silence, then Crowe said, 'The logical consequence would be an open verdict at the inquest.'

'I would doubt an open verdict, but without Richard to question, charge or prosecute, it could well be murder by a person or persons unknown.'

'Well, I regard that as totally unacceptable. It would have an appalling effect on the morale of this laboratory if it were to remain unresolved.'

'I can't imagine Harry Benedict being very happy either, Dr Crowe. After all, it could have a significant effect on him.'

'Yes, it could, couldn't it?' Crowe said in a more thoughtful tone. 'But the evidence still points *mostly* to Richard, doesn't it? And I don't believe the Coroner carries the same burden of proof as does the prosecution in the Criminal Court.'

'That will be for the Coroner's Court to decide.'

'Just so.' There was another short silence, then Crowe said, 'So, what do you intend doing, Mr Jones?'

'I'll need to talk to my superior before

anything else, but after that, I imagine we'll have to tell the Trust and the police about our findings.'

Crowe said, 'I'd appreciate it, Mr Jones—' his tone had become markedly more conciliatory—'if you could leave speaking to the Trust and the police until I've had a chance to speak to *my* superiors in London.'

Tom didn't say anything and he continued, 'You see, I have a legal obligation to—'

There was the briefest of knocks, then the door opened and an attractive and well-dressed woman of about thirty-five came in.

'Oh, I'm sorry, Theo. There was no one in the office downstairs and I didn't realise you had someone here.'

Tom got to his feet as Crowe said, 'Caroline, what ... ?' He recovered himself. 'We won't be much longer. If you could give us another minute ...'

Tom, realising from Crowe's discomfiture that he didn't want them to meet, said quickly, 'Oh, don't mind me—I think we were just about finished, weren't we, Dr Crowe?' He smiled at Caroline, who smiled back.

Crowe came out from behind his desk. 'Caroline, this is Mr Jones ... Mr Jones, my wife.'

'How d'you do?' Tom said politely.

'Hello. I'm so sorry to have interrupted you.'

'That's quite all right.' Knowing that his time was limited, he continued quickly, 'Just to summarise then, Dr Crowe, you'd like me to hold back from saying anything to the Trust or the police, until you've spoken to your head office?'

An awareness in Caroline's eyes showed that she realised what they were talking about.

'I would appreciate that, yes, Mr Jones.' Crowe's voice failed to conceal his irritation.

'I'll be on my way, then. Goodbye, Mrs Crowe.'

'Goodbye, Mr Jones.'

Outside the door, he paused, then walked slowly down the marble stairs, his brain racing.

Why didn't he want us to meet? He glanced at his watch: it was a little after eleven. *He wasn't expecting her, so she probably won't stay very long ...*

He reached the hall, sat down on one of the chairs. The receptionist was back now, even if she hadn't been there before. She caught his eye, and said, 'Can I help you, Mr Jones?'

'It's all right, thanks, I'm waiting for someone.'

He picked up a paper, looked at it without seeing ...

Five minutes passed and he was beginning to feel conspicuous, when he heard her footsteps on the stairs. He waited until she was in the hall before looking up, smiling and nodding to her. 'Mrs Crowe.'

She smiled back. 'Mr Jones.'

'Do allow me ...' He got up and opened the door for her.

'Thank you—my goodness!' she exclaimed. 'It's so bright out here.' She fumbled in her bag.

'Or dim inside, perhaps,' Tom said.

'Yes.' She found some dark glasses, put them on. Tom waited.

She said, 'I ... believe you've been to see Harry Benedict?'

Whatever Tom had been anticipating, it wasn't this. 'Yes, I did, yesterday.'

'How is he?'

'He's under a lot of strain, and showing it—which perhaps isn't really surprising under the circumstances.'

'No ...' She hesitated. 'Will you be seeing him again?'

'Yes, I will, this afternoon.'

'Would you please pass on my sympathy to him? And my—my regards?'

'Of course I will.'

'Thank you, Mr Jones.'

She walked over to her car, a black BMW, and got in. Started the engine, backed out and drove away. Tom watched until it was out of sight, then set off for his own car, which was in the main park.

Something made him turn and look up—and he was just in time to see the blind of Crowe's window move back into place.

18

'You'd better come in,' Harry said without enthusiasm and led Tom to the sitting-room. 'Have a seat. What's on your mind?' No offer of coffee this time.

'Whoever changed that result did it because they had it in for you.'

'I think I'd worked that out for myself.' He was dressed in denim as before and looked, if possible, even worse. 'And yes, Richard Kelso did have it in for me.'

Tom said, 'As I told you yesterday, there are two others besides Richard who've got it in for you. Now, I think there may be a third.'

'What d'you mean?'

'I met Mrs Crowe earlier this morning, Mrs Caroline Crowe. She asked me to pass on her sympathy to you. Also her regards.'

'Good of her.'

'Did you have an affair with her?'

'I don't think that's any of your business.'

'It is actually,' Tom said. 'Don't you want to know who killed your son?'

'I already know who killed my son— Richard Kelso.'

Tom leaned forward. 'I know that you *want* it to be, because if it wasn't, you're likely to be done for his murder. Me, I just want the truth.'

'The idea being, I suppose, that it was Crowe in a fit of jealousy?'

Tom didn't say anything.

'Yes, all right, I did have a brief fling with her, but there's no way Crowe could have known about it.'

'I wouldn't be so sure of that.'

Harry said, 'But I can't see how Crowe, or any of them, *could* have done it—changed the result, I mean. They may have been in the lab at the time, but they couldn't have known when to change it.'

'They could, as it happens.' Tom told him about his morning with Parker.

'All right,' Harry said, 'so maybe it's possible for someone who understands computers, but Crowe *doesn't* understand computers.'

'How d'you know that?'

'It's common knowledge.'

'Dr Crowe isn't as stupid as he likes to pretend.' Tom paused. 'What about Joy and Amina—how good are they with computers?'

'Joy's a bit better than Crowe, although that's not saying much.'

'And Amina?'

'She's pretty good.' It came out with a certain reluctance.

'Talking of Amina, she's asked me to pass a message on to you as well. She wants you to know that you're in her thoughts.'

Harry said, 'That's nice of her.'

'You don't know about Amina, then?' Tom said, watching him carefully.

'Know what about her?'

'She was attacked last night in the hospital, while she was on call.'

Harry stared at him a second, then fumbled for his cigarette pack. 'Who by?'

'I don't know. Nor do the police.'

Harry found a cigarette, lit it. 'Was she hurt?'

'Shaken more than anything.' He described her injuries. 'They're keeping her in for observation, though.'

'I'd go and see her, only I'm not allowed to go to the hospital.' He paused. 'Do the police think they'll catch them?'

'I don't know.'

'Some nutter, I expect, so probably not. I'll drop her a line.' He heaved in another lungful of smoke. 'But to come back to your theory that Amina or one of the others could've changed that result, that's all it is, a theory—and a pretty naff one at that. The *fact* remains that it was Richard who actually did it.'

Tom said, 'I'm not so sure about that any more. I still can't understand why, if it *was* Richard, he didn't simply put in the false result and pretend it was a mistake. Or why—'

'We've been over all this,' Harry said tiredly. 'He did it on impulse after he'd put in the right result.'

'—or why,' Tom continued, 'he left the right result pencilled on the path form for—'

'Because he *forgot*—and it's the police who say that, not just me.' He stubbed out his cigarette and fumbled for another. 'All I know is that when I saw his face that morning, I knew it was him. He was like a trapped animal.' He lit the fresh cigarette. 'Why are you so determined to show that it wasn't him?'

'I'm not, I just want the truth.' Tom let the silence hang a moment, then said, 'I met another acquaintance of yours yesterday.'

'Oh yes?'

'Your common law sister-in-law, Teresa.'

'Teresa—is she still around?'

'Why shouldn't she be?'

'I thought she was back at university. She's doing a degree in biomedical science —misguided idiot.'

'How did you and she get on?'

'All right. We rubbed along. Why?'

'Because she went to some trouble to find me and tell me that Richard Kelso couldn't have killed your son.'

There was a fraction's pause, then Harry burst out, 'How can she possibly say that?'

'She said that Richard loved Tania, and would never have harmed a child of hers. I found her rather persuasive.'

'You mean you *believed* her?'

'Both your assertions are highly subjective.'

Harry regarded him hollow-faced for a moment. 'Exactly what are you driving at, Mr Jones? Why are you here?'

'Because I want to know how much of your conviction that it was Richard is because it's to your advantage that way.'

Harry took a deep breath. 'All right, Mr Detective, let's play it your way, let's look at these *suspects*.' He drew on his cigarette. 'Crowe? Yeah, I humped his missus. She offered and I accepted. Why? 'Cos I felt like it and she don't get enough from him, I expect.'

Similar personalities ...? Tom thought. *God forbid!*

'Crowe doesn't know about me,' Harry continued, 'Caroline's too clever. But even if he *did*, he wouldn't—'

'How long ago was this fling?'

'About five months. She came round here to offer her condolences.' He shrugged. 'One offer led to another.'

'Before Amina, or during?'

'Before. Talking of Amina, you say she has reason to hate me, but the fact is, she doesn't—she just asked you to tell me I'm in her thoughts, didn't she?'

'Never heard of Oriental inscrutability?'

'Oriental bollocks—she was born in this country, she's no more Oriental than you or I.'

'Which leaves us with Joy ...'

'Well, Joy doesn't like me, that's for sure, but I still can't see her doing it.'

'And the reasons she doesn't like you are that you've undermined her, treated her with contempt and upset those members of staff she liked?'

'I couldn't have put it better myself.'

'So why do I get this feeling that her dislike of you runs deeper than that?'

'I don't know. You tell me.'

'Perhaps you've *humped* her as well.'

Harry looked at him incredulously. 'What, Megabum? I wouldn't touch her with yours.'

'Have you told her that?'

A heartbeat's pause. 'Yes, I suppose I have, in a manner of speaking.'

'Well, I'd say that could be more reason for her to hate you than all the others put together, wouldn't you?'

Harry shrugged again. 'I dunno. You're the great psychologist.'

Tom didn't say anything and after a pause, Harry continued, more slowly: 'It was after Tania was killed, not long before I went back to work. She came round one evening to see how I was getting on. She brought a bottle of wine.' He smiled a Toby jug smile. 'I remember thinking: *How nice ... we've been at each other's throats all this time, and now she's offering me friendship ...*' He looked up at Tom. 'You know something? I was actually touched, I really thought I was seeing a bit of human compassion, altruism. I wasn't, of course.' He let out a sigh.

'Well, we drank the wine, talked, and about eleven, I suddenly wanted to be on my own. Bereavement gets to you like that, you know, you suddenly *have* to be on your own.

'Anyway, I dropped subtle hints like: *I'm*

224

really knackered, that wine's really knocked me out, accompanied by yawns, and she said ... d'you know what she said?'

Tom shook his head.

'She said, *I expect the nights must feel lonely now* ... I ask you! Imagine waking up and finding that in bed next to you.' He rolled his eyes. *'Oh, Joy shall be yours in the morning ...'*

Tom smiled despite himself. 'Isn't it possible you misconstrued her?'

'Not a chance.'

'So you let her know what you thought of her offer?'

'No—I tried to let her down lightly, for me. Said I had to get up early to take Peter to Tania's parents, which was true, as it happened.'

'And she went?'

'Without a murmur. But she knew she was being turned down and she didn't like it. It made things worse between us when I did go back to work.'

'And promptly took up with Amina again.'

'Yeah—well, that didn't help much either.'

'I wonder if she really did come round out of sympathy, and then the wine, the talk, the intimacy, just got the better of her?'

Harry gave another shrug. 'Possible, I

suppose. All comes down to the same thing in the end though, doesn't it?'

'Whichever, it certainly gives her a motive.'

'Maybe, but still nothing like so strong as Richard's.'

'Never heard of the fury of a woman scorned?'

'I've been there,' Harry said with infinite weariness, 'done all that. And let me tell you something—it's all wind and piss, signifying nothing.'

Tom tried to swallow his rising anger. ''Course, you've scorned Amina twice now.'

'Yep.' No protestations of regret this time.

'So it's happy ever after with the nubile sister.'

'That's right. The girl of my wet dreams.'

Tom said slowly, 'Joy told me yesterday that you'd brought this tragedy on yourself.' He knew he shouldn't, but he couldn't stop himself. 'At the time I thought she was being rather hard on you, but I can see now what she meant.'

Harry said softly, 'Get out of my house.' Amina would have recognised the tone in his voice.

Tom stood up. 'The real tragedy being

that it was your son who was killed. I'll see myself out.' He made for the door—then tried to turn as he heard Harry behind him.

He was too late, a hand shoved him forward ... he staggered, came upright.

Harry's left fist flickered at his face. Tom began raising his arms, then swivelled sideways as Harry's right snaked into his midriff.

He staggered again, winded, but not that badly ... he clutched his stomach, gasping.

Harry relaxed. 'Get out.'

Tom straightened and kicked for his crotch in a single movement, but Harry saw it coming and took it on the thigh.

They faced each other, two London alley cats, spitting, hair on end, claws unsheathed.

For five long seconds, they stared at each other, each aware they were evenly matched, then Harry said again, 'Get out of my house.'

Tom held the stare for three more seconds, then felt for the door handle behind him and backed out of the room.

On the pavement, he found he was trembling ... before he had time to think, a green Rover pulled in beside him and Sally Yate climbed out.

'Hello, Mr Jones.'

'Hello.'

'Are you coming or going?' she asked.

'Going,' Tom said.

'Are you all right? What's happened?'

'Nothing.' He forced a smile. 'Nothing's happened.'

'Have you and Harry had a row or something?'

Tom shrugged. 'Just words.'

She regarded him a moment. 'Mr Jones, Harry's been under the most unbelievable stress the last few days, as I'm sure you can understand. He simply isn't in his right mind at the moment—I hope you can understand that.'

'I *am* aware of the strain he's been under, but he's not doing himself any favours at the moment.'

'I know that.'

'Then you might try getting it across to him ... Sorry, I know it's not your fault.'

She watched as he got into his car and drove off.

He drove a little way out of the village and, still shaken, pulled in under some trees and lit a cheroot.

After the smoke had calmed him, he found himself wondering again what it was that Sally could possibly see in him. *Is she mothering him?* he wondered, remembering what Amina had said. Sally didn't look exactly motherly ... and as for Benedict, there was something deeply wrong there.

He finished the cheroot and drove off. He was just entering the suburbs when his mobile phone went. He flipped the switch on the dash.

'Hello?'

'Tom, it's Marcus.'

'Let me find somewhere to stop, Marcus.'

He turned down a side street, pulled in and lifted the receiver from its cradle.

'Hello.'

'Tom, what have you been doing to upset Dr Crowe?'

Tom let out a groan. 'I've added him to my lists of suspects, that's what. Why, what's happened?'

'He's been on to Mrs Castleton, complaining that you've been exceeding your brief and making wild accusations about his staff.'

'The bastard!' Tom spluttered. 'He asked me to hold off speaking to her myself so that he could talk to his head office.'

'Well, apparently, he was going to complain to the police as well, but Mrs C's persuaded him not to for the moment.'

'I wouldn't bank on that.'

'Why have you added him to your list?'

Tom told him about Mrs Crowe.

'Are there any women down there that Benedict *hasn't* had?' Marcus asked wonderingly.

'Yes, there is one as a matter of fact—Joy Manners, his boss. And according to him, she was somewhat piqued about it.' He related Harry's story. 'Of course, we'd probably get a completely different version from her.'

'Don't ask her, Tom, whatever you do.' He paused. 'Have you spoken to all the people you wanted to yet?'

'Pretty well—oh, there is one I'll need to see again.' He told him about Teresa and his conviction she was hiding something.

'She'll need careful handling by the sound of it,' Marcus said.

'Yes. And there's Crowe himself of course, I'll have to think of a way of smoking him out.'

'Well, that shouldn't be too difficult with those filthy things of yours. Seriously, Tom,' he continued, 'don't go near Crowe or any of them for the moment.' He paused again. 'I wonder if I ought to come down myself.'

'Let me sit down and think about what I've got first,' Tom said, he hoped not too quickly.

'All right. I'll speak to you later this afternoon.'

19

Tom had been nagging the Home Office for years, so far in vain, to develop a mini version of HOLMES that would run on laptop; in the meantime, he'd developed his skills at making flow charts to an extent to make it almost unnecessary.

After a sandwich in the bar, he went up to his room, made a pot of coffee and went carefully through all the notes he'd taken. Then he began constructing a chart for Crowe, Joy, Amina and Richard, including every event he'd been told about, together with its time and source, so that he could compare them all directly. He was pondering the result an hour later when the phone went.

'Jones.'

'It's Liz Kendall, here, Tom.' She sounded strangely formal despite the Christian names. 'I'm phoning to tell you, officially, that you must drop your enquiries for the time being.'

'Crowe?'

'Pardon? Oh, yes—he complained to the super about half an hour ago and he told me to tell you.'

'Good of him. Listen, Liz,' he continued before she could say anything, 'I've got some new evidence I think you should see. Can you come over?'

'Can't you tell me over the phone?'

'Not really, no.'

There was a pause. 'All right, I'll be with you as soon as I can.'

Tom told reception he was expecting her, then rather self-consciously tidied his room. She arrived a quarter of an hour later.

'You don't seem very surprised,' he said after he'd told her about Caroline Crowe and Harry.

She shrugged. 'Not really. Benedict's clearly one of those men women find irresistible. No, really,' she said, seeing the look on his face, 'he does have sex appeal.'

Tom gave a snort of disgust and she grinned impishly at him. 'Jealous?'

'Of Benedict? Never in a million light years.'

Still smiling, she said, 'Well, I suppose if Dr Crowe is similarly unmoved, it gives him a motive. What's this?'

She pointed to the flow chart and Tom explained it to her. She listened intently, not interrupting. When he'd finished, she said, 'So while Richard Kelso was on the phone, we have Crowe alone with a terminal in his office, Joy in hers and Amina maybe in the reception office ... why d'you go for Crowe and not one of the others?'

Tom took a breath, released it. 'I suppose it comes down to the gut feeling that Joy and Amina were telling me the truth—more or less, anyway—and that Crowe wasn't.'

'But is his motive really any stronger than the others?'

'You haven't met him, Liz. He's a very proud man, arrogant, and being cuckolded by Benedict is probably about the worst insult that could be inflicted on him.'

'But that's just your opinion, surely?'

'There's something I'd forgotten.' He stared at her. 'He was consulted that night about Peter, remember? So he was able to make sure the wrong treatment was maintained.'

'I'd forgotten that too,' she said.

'From the moment I arrived he's been pressurising me to agree that it was Kelso. He was really rattled when his wife interrupted us, and then spied on us when she asked me to give Benedict a message.'

'And then complained to us about your handling of things,' she said thoughtfully.

'Exactly.'

'Are you sure you're not prejudiced? I mean, you don't like him much, do you?'

'I don't like any of them much, except perhaps Amina.'

'Who, of the three, has the best understanding of computers, a pretty strong motive and was found lurking near a computer terminal.' She paused, looked at the chart again.

'You know, Tom,' she said at last, 'if I was the Coroner, looking at this, I'd still have to say that Richard Kelso was the most likely person.'

'What about the pencilled result that worried you so much earlier?'

'The balance of his mind, and so on. I'm being the superintendent, it'll be him in the box, not me.'

'What about Teresa Belling telling me that he couldn't have done it?'

'But failing to produce any evidence.'

'She's hiding something, Liz, I'm sure of it.'

Liz said, 'I think it's time I talked to her myself. What's her address?'

'I'll come with you.'

She shook her head. 'I don't think so, Tom.'

He said carefully, 'Liz, with respect, I think she'll just clam up if you go on your own.'

She considered him a moment, then nodded. 'All right.'

Remembering how she'd fled the night before, Tom suggested they go straight to her parents' house without phoning first. It was a large Victorian semi in a quiet cul-de-sac, and the door was opened by a small grey-haired woman somehow made smaller by the sadness etched in her face.

'Mrs Belling?' Liz asked.

'Yes?'

She showed her identification. 'Could we speak to Teresa, please?'

'I'm afraid she's not here at the moment ... although she should be back at any minute.'

Liz gave her an abridged version of why they were there and she asked them in to wait. Teresa arrived ten minutes later to find them ensconced in the front room with cups of tea.

She glared at Tom mutinously. 'I told you all I could last night. There's nothing else.'

Liz said, 'Miss Belling, please listen to what we have to say, just for a few minutes.'

'I don't think a few minutes would hurt, dear,' said her mother. 'They did say it was important.'

Teresa knew when she was outmanoeuvred. 'All right, a few minutes. Alone, Mum,' she added pointedly.

Mrs Belling reluctantly left them and

Teresa went over to the big bay window, where she stood silhouetted in the light.

'Well?'

Tom said, 'When you came to see me last night, I'd more or less accepted, along with everybody else, that Richard Kelso killed your nephew. Now, I'm not so sure, but we can't take it any further unless you give us a better reason than just that you *know*.'

'Well, I'm sorry, but I can't.'

'Can't or won't?'

'Can't.'

'All the evidence we have points to Richard. His colleagues, even those who liked him, think he did it. And yet you say you *know* that he didn't.'

She regarded him sullenly.

'I don't believe you could be that certain unless there's something you didn't tell me.'

'I can't.' She swallowed. 'I gave my word.'

'To whom—Richard?'

'No.'

'Tania, then?'

She nodded.

Liz said, 'Unless you can give us reason to the contrary, Richard Kelso will take the blame for this killing, whatever we may think.'

'But there'd be an open verdict, surely?'

'No,' Tom said. 'Either Richard will be named as the killer, or it will be murder by a person or persons unknown—in which case, everyone would assume it was Richard.'

'Does it *matter?*' she said wildly. 'He's dead, isn't he?'

'It mattered to you yesterday,' he reminded her.

'I gave my *word*, can't you understand that?'

'It's not just that an innocent dead person would be blamed,' said Liz, 'but that a live, *guilty* one would get away with it. And might do it again,' she added.

She sat down, stared at the carpet. Moments passed.

'All right,' she said at last.

'What did Tania tell you, Teresa?' Liz asked gently.

Still staring at the floor, Teresa began speaking in a low voice.

'She—she told me after Peter was born that ... that Harry wasn't his natural father. Richard was.' She raised her eyes. 'Now d'you see? Richard wouldn't have killed his own son, would he?'

Tom and Liz stared at each other a moment, then Liz turned back to her. 'But did Richard *know* this?'

'Yes. Apparently, he'd guessed.'

'*Apparently* ...?'

'Tania told me that he challenged her with it. She denied it, but he refused to believe her.' Now that she'd decided to talk, it was coming more easily.

'So Richard didn't tell you any of this himself?'

'Not until after Tania was killed, no.'

'But he told you then?'

She nodded. 'It's why he was so wretched. He would have liked to have brought Peter up himself.'

'Did he actually tell you that?'

'Yes, and he meant it.'

'When did he tell you?' Tom asked.

'Oh, several times—he'd become a bit obsessed about it. I suppose the last time was about two weeks ago.'

'And that was the last time you spoke to him?'

'No.' Her eyes and lips clamped shut a moment. 'It was me who told him that Peter was dead. I rang him on the Saturday after Harry phoned us here ...' She found a tissue, dabbed at her eyes. 'I thought I owed it to Richard to tell him myself.'

Resisting the urge to glance at Liz again, Tom said, 'What time did you ring him?'

'Oh, just after Harry phoned at eight.'

'What did he say when you told him?'

'He seemed to take it very calmly.

He asked me for the details, which I gave him.'

Casually, so as not to arouse her suspicions, Tom said, 'Didn't Harry ever suspect that Peter wasn't his son?'

'Tania said not. Peter was like her, you see. Harry never gave any sign that he knew.'

'Didn't he guess?' said Liz. 'Dates and so forth.'

Teresa sighed. 'I know this doesn't show Tania in a very good light, but she was very confused and muddled at the time ... there were about two weeks when she was sleeping with them both.'

'So how could *she* know which of them was the father?'

Teresa smiled, sadly. 'I asked her that. She said she just knew. It's something women know, she said.'

20

The snap as Tom fastened his seat belt seemed unnaturally loud. 'Well, that changes things a bit,' he said, 'doesn't it?'

Liz snorted. 'That must be the understatement of the millennium.' She continued more slowly, 'It comes down to whether or not Benedict knew ...'

'Liz, she's watching us, I think we'd better go.'

She started the engine and slowly drove off. 'So how do we go about finding out whether he knew?'

'I'm thinking,' Tom said. 'Something Amina told me ... Benedict works with DNA identification.'

'So it's possible he could have found out for himself.' She indicated, changed down and turned, inserting herself into the stream of traffic on the main road. 'But would he have killed Peter, just because he was Richard Kelso's son?'

'Well, we thought Richard had killed him just because he was Benedict's son.'

'Yes, but Peter hadn't actually lived with Richard, had he? I just can't believe ...' She let out a sigh. 'And besides, Benedict *couldn't* have done it, he wasn't anywhere near the computer, was he?'

'He was in the Children's Ward,' Tom said slowly.

'And there's a terminal in the duty room,' Liz said. 'Could he have done it from there?'

'According to Chris Parker, from anywhere in the region ... and Katie Ashfield told me ...' Tom scrabbled for his notebook. 'Yes, here it is, Sister was called away to Ward B, Dr Miller wasn't around. Katie took the call from the lab, then Benedict came out of Peter's room demanding to know what was going on, she told him the lab was on the phone ...'

'And then left him in the duty room with the terminal,' Liz completed. 'But he wouldn't have done it there for everyone to see, surely?'

'There was no one else actually in the duty room at that time,' said Tom, 'just the staff nurse in one of the cubicles. It depends how long he was out there ... The nanny, did you talk to the nanny?'

'N—no ...'

'Marie something ...' He flicked a couple of pages. 'Marie Davidson. She'll know how long he was out of the room. And then there's the fact that he actually killed Richard Kelso—the *bastard*—'

'Tom, we don't know that it was him, we don't even know whether what Teresa told us was true yet.'

'That's easy enough. Arrange DNA profiles on Peter and Richard—how long would that take?'

'At least four days,' she said. 'More likely a week.'

'We need something sooner than that ... Blood groups, I think you can do it with blood groups. Can I use your mobile?'

'I'm pulling in if you're going to start phoning people,' she said. 'I don't know where I was going, anyway.'

She parked in a side street as Tom found the number he wanted and punched it in.

'Mrs Castleton? It's Tom Jones here ...'

A few minutes later, he gently replaced it. 'Well, she doesn't like it, but she knows Dr Forester, the consultant haematologist, and will see what she can do. Now, the next thing's the nanny ...' He picked the mobile up again.

'You're a proper little bloodhound once you get going, aren't you?' Liz said.

Tom had got Marie's number from Directory Enquiries and they were on their way to see her. He shrugged modestly.

'Or maybe more of a terrier,' she continued. 'Yes, a terrier that's smelt a rat.'

'Well, we've certainly done that.'

'There's one thing I still don't understand—why did Benedict go to the lab on Saturday? It's obvious now why Kelso did, but why Benedict?'

'I wonder—' began Tom, but was interrupted by the mobile. He picked it up.

'Speaking ... oh yes, Mrs Castleton ...'

He listened intently for a while, then said, 'That's great, thanks very much.' He replaced it and turned to Liz. 'You can show a ninety-nine per cent probability using blood-grouping tests, which'll be enough for you to take to Southey.'

'How are they going to get the blood from—?'

'Well, we're in luck there, the mortuary always take samples and store them. We should have a result in a couple of hours. Now let's concentrate on the nanny.'

'It's the *you to take to Southey* bit I don't like.'

Tom grinned at her. 'Oh, just flutter your eyelashes at him and you'll be all right.'

'Thanks,' she said drily.

Marie lived on the other side of the village from Harry, in a small but smart bungalow.

'Inspector Kendall and Mr Jones? Do come in.' She led them to a comfortable living-room where Liz gave her the authorised version of why they were there.

'We're trying to get as broad a picture as we can of what happened that Friday, Mrs Davidson, so if you could tell us what you remember about it ...'

With gentle prompting, Marie went through the events of the day, her voice level and unemotional until she came to the evening.

'It was obvious he was getting worse,

but they wouldn't listen to me. They were busy, they said he was bound to get a bit worse before he got better, they clearly thought I was an interfering old busybody. I'm not saying it was their fault,' she added hastily, 'they're overworked and there aren't enough of them, but if they'd paid more attention to me, perhaps ...' She stopped herself with an effort. 'Anyway, at about a quarter past five, I found Dr Miller and made such a fuss that he came and looked at Peter and then got on to the lab to read the Sensitivity Test.'

'When did Mr Benedict arrive?' Liz asked.

'I'm not sure exactly, about half-past five, I think. I'll never forget his face, it was so grim. Peter was crying, whimpering in pain ...' She pulled a handkerchief from her sleeve, wiped her eyes. 'Then Mr Benedict said he couldn't stand it any longer and was going to find out what was going on. When he came back, he said the lab had phoned, but wouldn't speak to anyone except Sister, who'd been called away.'

'Did he say who told him that?'

'The student nurse, Katie, who'd gone to look for her. I was furious. He said it was something to do with the ward losing messages; anyway, then Sister came back, Dr Miller started the new treatment, and at about a quarter past six, Mr Benedict told me that everything was going to be all right and that I was to go home. I wish I hadn't ... I can't believe how that man Kelso, how *anyone* could be so evil ... I'm sorry ...'

'Don't be,' Liz said quietly. 'I'm sorry to have brought it all back to you.'

When she'd recovered a little, Tom said, 'So many things seem to have been happening at the time the lab phoned—Sister being called away and the nurse going to look for her, the doctor not being there—we're finding it very difficult to understand exactly what was going on.'

'I'm not surprised, it was very confusing.'

'Let me run through it with you to make sure I've got it right.' He consulted his notebook. 'Dr Miller looked at Peter at about 5.15 and then asked the lab to do the test?'

'Yes.'

'Mr Benedict arrived at about 5.30?'

'Yes.'

'Sister was called away, Dr Miller wasn't there, the lab rang and Nurse Ashfield went to look for Sister?'

'Yes ... I didn't see any of that happening—Mr Benedict told me.'

'Of course. Mr Benedict went into the duty room at about 5.35 to find out what was going on and returned, what? Two or three minutes later?'

'I didn't think it was as long as that …'

'A minute or two, then?'

'Yes, all right.'

'And then Sister came back and answered the phone?'

'Yes,' she said. 'I can't be exact about these times.'

'That's understood, so long as they're about right. Then Dr Miller came back and the new treatment was started?'

'Yes.'

'Thank you very much, Mrs Davidson.' He shut his notebook and smiled at her. 'That gives us a much clearer idea.'

'Inconclusive, I'm afraid, Tom,' Liz said as they drove away. 'A good defence lawyer could easily bring that minute or two down to a few seconds.'

'But I've shown that changing the result would only *take* a few seconds.'

'In the middle of a duty room where someone was liable to come in any minute? I'm being devil's advocate.'

'He'd have said he was looking up his son's results, which would have been perfectly natural—and, Liz, I think I know why he went into the lab on Saturday now.'

'I'm listening.'

'For exactly the same reason we thought Richard had—because he'd remembered something and wanted to cover it up.'

'Remembered what?'

'If we knew that,' Tom said, 'I think it would clinch things.'

Liz nodded slowly, changing down as she approached the main road. 'So he killed Richard to prevent him finding whatever it was?'

'No, I think Richard got there first and had already found it.'

He watched her profile as she both concentrated on her driving and measured his words.

'But *would* Richard have got there first?' she said.

'Oh yes, he'd have wanted to check whether he'd made a mistake, so he'd have gone in the moment Teresa told him.'

'But wouldn't Benedict have gone in straight away as well?'

'Not necessarily, maybe he remembered whatever it was a little while after he'd phoned the Bellings ...'

'And meanwhile, Richard found it and accused Benedict when he arrived?'

'Yes—he'd have seen the false result on the computer and known *he* hadn't put it there, then he'd have remembered where Benedict was when he phoned the ward ...

in fact, he might have actually overheard Benedict talking to Nurse Ashfield then heard her say she was going to look for Sister. Leaving Benedict with a computer terminal ...'

They reached the outskirts of the town. 'I'm sure you're right, Tom,' Liz said. 'But without witnesses, or some other hard evidence, it's not going to be easy to prove.'

'No ...'

There was nothing else they could do until they heard from Mrs Castleton, so they drove to the seafront, tossed a few more ideas about without getting anywhere.

Liz was looking out to sea. She said, 'You know something, I never get tired of this view.'

The sand on the beach gleamed in the sun, the sea sparkled and the distant cliffs, fading into the September mist, seemed to assume the mystery of mountains.

'I don't think I would, on a day like this.' Tom was feeling completely at ease with her now, just enjoying her presence. He took out his cheroots.

'Not in the car, you don't,' she said equably.

He grinned sheepishly and opened the door. He'd just lit up when the mobile went.

Liz picked it up. 'It's for you,' she said.

He put out the cheroot, took it and listened. 'Yes ... yes ... thank you very much, Mrs Castleton.' He turned to Liz. 'Richard Kelso was Peter Benedict's natural father—at least, so far as blood groups go.'

'Let's go and find the superintendent —and I do mean *us*, Tom. I need the moral support.'

Southey listened with pursed lips.

'I do seem to remember telling you that the enquiry was to be dropped,' he said when Liz finished.

'Yes, sir, you did, but in the light of the new evidence Mr Jones gave me, I thought ...'

'All right, inspector. You've made a good case—the thing is, do we wait for DNA confirmation, or bring him in on the strength of the blood tests?' He pondered a moment. 'I think I'd better have a word with Dr Forester myself.' He made a note on his pad. 'The crucial question is whether or not Benedict *knew* he wasn't Peter's real father—that's what it hinges on.'

'He does work with DNA identification,' Tom reminded him.

'So you said, but would he have been

able to do a DNA profile himself?'

'I don't know.'

'I'll speak to Dr Crowe about that, tonight if possible.' Another note. 'Thank you, Mr Jones you can leave it with us now.'

Tom realised he was being dismissed.

'What d'you think you'll do, superintendent?' he asked. 'Bring him in?'

'I haven't made up my mind yet. I think on balance I probably will—he is still on bail after all, so it won't be any problem.'

'Is there anything I can do to help?'

Southey considered him. 'Yes, there is as a matter of fact. Find out exactly what it was that took Benedict to the lab on Saturday morning.'

21

'This is Interview Room Two at Regis Central Police Station and I am Detective Superintendent John Southey of the Dorset Constabulary. It is 1100 hours on Saturday 30th September and we are here to interview Mr Harry Benedict. I will now ask the others in the room to identify themselves. Mr Benedict?'

Harry cleared his throat. 'Harry James Benedict.'

'Thank you, Mr Benedict. Inspector?'

'I am Inspector Elizabeth Jane Kendall of the Dorset Constabulary.'

Southey and Harry faced each other across a table, which was set against the wall of the windowless room. The tape recorder was between them and Liz sat on the third side. Southey turned to the fourth person in the room.

'Mr Larsen?'

'I am Christopher Larsen, solicitor representing Mr Harry Benedict. And I wish to have it on record that I object to the fact that my chair has been fixed to the floor in a position which makes it very difficult to communicate with my client.'

'As I explained to you earlier, Mr Larsen, the furniture in this room is fixed, as it is in all of our interview rooms, for reasons of safety, in accordance with the Health and Safety Act of 1974.'

No one had ever yet actually checked the Health and Safety Act 1974 to see whether this was strictly true and Southey hoped that it wouldn't occur to Larsen to do so now. It *was* true that an interviewee had once jumped to his feet before anyone could stop him and swung his chair at Southey's head.

It was also true that it suited Southey

very well to have Larsen fixed in a position two yards behind Harry, so that they couldn't make eye contact. More than one suspect in the past had blurted something out before his solicitor could stop him.

'Now, Mr Benedict, we've asked you here to clarify certain of the points you made in your previous statement. On the Saturday following your son's death, you told us that you telephoned your late partner's parents, to inform them of Peter's death, at about eight o'clock in the morning?'

'Yes.'

'And that afterwards, you felt there was something *wrong* about your son's death and drove to the laboratory?'

'That's right, yes.'

'What time would that have been?'

'Twenty, twenty-five past eight. We have been over all this before, superintendent.'

'Could you tell us again, please, sir?'

Slowly, laboriously Harry did so.

Southey and Liz had carefully planned the interview to ensure that Harry repeated all the statements they now knew to be untrue; also to induce a sense of complacency in him.

Teresa had made a statement confirming that Richard had known Peter was his son, although she hadn't wavered in her belief that Harry hadn't known. However,

Southey's talk with Dr Crowe had yielded another very interesting fact ...

'So, to summarize,' Southey said, 'you drove to the laboratory, went inside and saw Kelso on the stairs, he shouted something like *bastard* and attacked you?'

'Yes.'

'And in defending yourself in the ensuing fight, you inadvertently killed him?'

'Yes.'

'And you think he attacked you because you'd disturbed him while he was attempting to cover up the fact that he'd put the false result into the computer which led to your son's death?'

'That's right, yes.'

'Thank you.' He turned to Liz. 'Inspector?'

'Mr Benedict, I'd like to go over with you the period of time when you were with your son, Peter, and Mrs Marie Davidson, his nanny, on the Children's Ward, while Mr Kelso was reading the Direct Sensitivity Test.'

'All right,' Harry said. His eyes flickered as he thought for a moment, then he began speaking again ...

He was standing up well to the questioning so far; he looked at ease and his answers were natural and spontaneous. He hadn't realised yet that Richard's death was not the main subject of the interview.

Liz was saying, 'According to your previous statement, you left Room Three, your son Peter's room, and went out into the duty room at about 5.35—is that correct?'

'Yes.'

'Why did you do that?'

'Because Peter was clearly very distressed and I wanted to find out what was holding things up.'

'And did you find out?'

'Yes, the nurse there told me the lab was on the phone and she was on her way to find Sister.'

'Then what happened?'

'She left and I went back into Peter's room.'

'And there was no one else in the duty room at the time?'

'No—although there was a staff nurse in with one of the other patients.'

'How long would you say you had been out of your son's room?'

Harry made a mouth. 'Half a minute. If that.'

'Oh? Mrs Davidson has told us it was longer than that.'

Harry's eyes flicked up. 'Then she was mistaken.'

'Nevertheless, that's what she says.'

Harry said, 'Well, we were neither of us watching the clock just then, and we did have other things to worry about. Anyway, I still can't see that it was much over half a minute.'

'All right. Then what happened?'

'Sister came back and answered the phone, then she bleeped Dr Miller and called up the results on the computer.'

'You saw this for yourself?'

'I saw Dr Miller at the nurses' station, went out, and he showed me the results. I thought then that our troubles were over,' he added.

'Because the doctor now knew the best drug with which to treat your son?'

'That's right.'

Liz looked at Southey, who took over the questioning again.

'Mr Benedict, you told us in your last statement why it was that Richard Kelso hated you so much, hated you enough, in fact, to want to harm you by harming your son.'

'Yes?'

'I'd like to touch on a few of the points you made about that ...'

The lengthy questioning was beginning to tell on Harry now. He lit a cigarette, watched the smoke spiralling up to the extractor vent of the windowless room.

'And so to recapitulate,' Southey said at last, 'Richard Kelso hated you when his fiancée, Tania, broke off their engagement to go and live with you, hated you even more when your son, Peter, was born, and then hated you more than ever when Tania was killed six months after that?'

'Yes.' Harry blew smoke.

'You haven't told us anything about your own feelings. Did you not hate him?'

'Well, I didn't like him much, obviously. He made life difficult for me whenever he could.'

'But *he* hated *you* so much that when he was suddenly presented with the opportunity to harm, to *kill*, your son Peter, he did so in order to harm you?'

'Yes.' Harry drew on the cigarette again, then stubbed it out in the tray.

'Well, Mr Benedict—' Southey sat back in his chair, looking directly into Harry's eyes— 'the reason we've asked you here today is because we've acquired some very interesting new evidence.'

There was a profound silence as they looked at each other across the table.

'We now know,' Southey continued, 'that there is a ninety-nine per cent chance that Peter Benedict was not, in fact, your son. He was the natural son of Richard Kelso.'

Harry's face drained, and then slowly, like a tide, flooded red. 'How did ...? I don't believe you ... Are you sure ...?'

Larsen's eyes snapped open and he sat

up in his chair. 'Don't say any more for the moment, Harry. Do you have this evidence in writing, superintendent?'

'I do.'

'May I see it?'

'Certainly.' Southey took a sheet of paper from the folder in front of him and handed it over. Larsen studied it carefully. Southey studied Harry. Harry looked down at the table in front of him, his lips compressed in a tight line.

Larsen looked up. 'This evidence is incomplete. Dr Forester says that it is not complete proof and that a DNA test must be done.'

'That is so, and the matter is in hand. And if it turns out that the ninety-nine per cent chance is wrong and the one per cent right, then I shall be the first to apologise to Mr Benedict. But I don't think that's very likely, do you, Mr Larsen?'

'I think we should wait and see, superintendent. In fact, I think that this interview should be suspended, as of now, until the DNA test is complete.'

'That is noted, Mr Larsen, but we have been here for only ninety minutes so far and there are some more questions I wish to put to Mr Benedict.'

'And I should like to be able to confer with him in private first.'

'You will be able to do so shortly, Mr

Larsen. Mr Benedict ...'

Harry slowly raised his head.

'You said just now that you didn't believe us—do I take that to mean that you didn't realise that Peter ... *might* not be your son?'

'I had no idea ...'

'Harry, don't say any more,' Larsen said.

'You had no idea, Mr Benedict?'

'None.'

'In that case, why, six months ago, did you send two samples of human blood to DNAscan Laboratories in Oxfordshire with a request for DNA profiling?'

Harry looked back at him. 'How ... ?'

'How did we know? Because you sent the samples under the auspices of your laboratory, and the Director there is a friend of Dr Crowe's. Well, Mr Benedict, why did you send them?'

Oh, you stupid wanker ... Harry thought.

Larsen said, 'You don't have to answer, Harry.'

'It's all right,' said Harry in a tired voice. 'It's true, I did know.'

'Are you now saying that you *did* know that Peter Benedict was not your natural son, Mr Benedict?'

'Yes.'

'Then why did you tell us earlier that you didn't know?'

'Is it the sort of thing you'd want to admit, superintendent?'

'I think in a matter as grave as this, I would, yes.'

'Well, *I* didn't.'

'Superintendent,' Larsen said loudly and clearly, 'I wish to confer with my client in private.'

'In just a moment, Mr Larsen. Mr Benedict, you do see, don't you, that this ... casts doubt, shall we say, on Richard Kelso's motive for killing Peter?'

Harry's eyes hunted around. 'But only if *he* knew ...'

'But he did know. We have a statement from Miss Teresa Belling, Tania's sister, in which she says that he did know that Peter was—'

'The *bitch!*'

'Harry, be quiet!'

'The thing is, Mr Benedict,' Southey continued unperturbed, 'it seems to us now, in the light of this new evidence, that in fact *you* had a stronger motive for killing Peter than—'

'*Me!* What absolute bollocks—'

'Harry, be *quiet.*'

'Anyway, how could I have done? I wasn't anywhere near the lab at the time.'

'There's a computer terminal in the duty room, to which you would have had access when Student Nurse Ashfield left.'

Harry tried to laugh. 'You must be out of your tiny minds if that's what you think.'

'Harry!'

'It also seems to us that you had a motive for killing Richard Kelso—'

Harry leapt to his feet. 'You *fuckers,* you're trying to fit me up—'

'Harry—sit *down!*' Larsen was on his feet now, his hands on Harry's shoulders. Liz was also standing. Harry slowly sank back on to his seat.

Larsen said, 'Superintendent, I demand to be allowed to confer with my client in private.'

'All right,' said Southey. 'Interview suspended at ...' He looked up at the clock. '1245 hours at the request of Mr Larsen.' He reached over and switched off the machine, then looked back at Larsen. 'I'd say you had quite a lot to talk about.'

22

The previous evening, Tom had persuaded Chris Parker to go to the microbiology lab with him, where they tried to work out what it was that had brought Harry in the previous Saturday.

They got nowhere—not then, nor later in the bar, nor even during the night in dreams.

'It'll come to you,' Marcus told him the next morning over the phone, 'probably when you least expect it. Get some fresh air, think about something else and it'll come.'

After lunch, heedful of this advice, Tom stuffed the mobile into his coat pocket, walked over to the pier, paid his pound and walked slowly along to the end of it.

Sunlight flashed from wavetops whipped up by a fresh sou'westerly, and salty water sucked and gurgled amongst the rusty iron piles below. Fishermen reeled in their lines and solemnly inspected their baits before recasting them, and distance somehow lent an elegance to the skyline of hotels across the water. It all seemed so fresh and healthy compared with the sordid mess he'd been working on ...

The mobile rang. He extracted it and took it into a wind shelter.

'Mr Jones?'

He groaned inwardly as he recognised the voice. 'Speaking.'

'It's Sally Yate here. Sister Yate.'

'Hello, Sister.' He felt as much as saw the hostile glances from the other occupants of the shelter.

'Mr Jones, Harry's been arrested, did you know that?'

'I had been told, yes.'

'His solicitor's just phoned me—they've accused him of killing Peter! They seem to think he changed the computer result himself, while he was here in the duty room.'

'Yes, I'd heard.'

'It's ridiculous! Apart from anything else, it would have been physically impossible.'

Why had she phoned *him*, wasn't she aware of his part in Harry's arrest? Perhaps not ...

She continued, 'There are two people with me now, Dr Miller and Staff Nurse Radford, who were here in the duty room at the time and saw Harry talking to Nurse Ashfield. Will you come and listen to what they have to say? Please, Mr Jones.'

'All right,' he said. It would probably be emotional and embarrassing, but he'd better. 'Give me half an hour.'

In fact, it was twenty-nine minutes later when he pushed the intercom button at the ward entrance and the familiar, slightly adenoidal voice replied,

'Children's Ward A, Student Nurse Ashfield ...'

He told her who he was and she let him in.

Sally was waiting by the nurses' station

with Jane Radford and Dr Miller, the latter looking slightly sheepish. There was no sign of Katie.

'Mr Jones, thank you for coming so quickly.' She was pale, strained, looked older somehow. She introduced Jane and Miller, then said, 'They were both here on the Friday when the call came from the microbiology lab. They know who you are and what the situation is.'

A worried-looking man—a parent, Tom assumed—came out of one of the cubicles. 'Sister, could you spare a minute, please?'

'Excuse me,' she said, and went over to him.

'Shall we find somewhere more private?' Tom said to the others.

'We'll be all right here,' Miller said, and led the way over to a bench seat by the corridor.

'Who wants to start?' Tom said when they'd sat down.

Jane and Miller looked at each other, then Jane said, 'I will.' She moistened her lips. 'I was in Room Six—' she indicated the cubicle the man had just come out of, which was opposite Peter's— 'changing the dressing on Sarah Paget and I asked Dr Miller to come and have a look at her, which he did. After he'd gone to the doctors' office to check up on what I'd shown him, I noticed Mr Benedict come

263

out of Room Three and talk to Nurse Ashfield. When I looked up again, the duty room was empty. I'm quite sure I'd have noticed if Mr Benedict had done anything with the computer.'

'How long was the interval between the times you looked up?'

'About half a minute.'

'Half a minute—are you certain of that?'

'As certain as I can be, yes.'

Her calm voice and untroubled grey eyes would make her a good witness, Tom realised. *That's bloody done it,* he thought, looking round with a desperation he tried to hide—then he had a flash of inspiration.

'Could you see into *all* of the duty room?' he asked. 'Around the murals?' He indicated the designs on the glass doors.

'Murals? Oh, I see what you mean ... I think so, yes.'

'Could you see into Peter's room?'

'Er—no.' She smiled. 'A mural too many.'

Tom smiled back. 'So you don't really know whether Mr Benedict had, in fact, gone back in there?'

'I ... suppose not. I don't know where else he could have gone, though.'

'Could you see up the corridor?' He indicated.

'N—no, I couldn't.'

'Did you see him again at all at around that time?'

'Not until after Sister and Dr Miller were back, no.'

'OK.' Tom made a few notes in his book. Sally came back and silently rejoined them. Tom turned to Miller. 'What about you, doctor?'

Miller glanced at Sally. 'I'm not sure how much this really helps.' He took a breath. 'After I'd asked the lab to read Peter's test and Sister had been called away, Jane—Staff Nurse Radford—asked me to have a look at Sarah Paget, as she told you. I didn't like the look of the wound and went along to the doctors' office to check up on it. By the time I'd found the information I needed, both Sister and Nurse Ashfield were back at the nurses' station.'

'So you didn't actually see Mr Benedict at all?'

'No, I'm afraid I didn't.'

'Where is the doctors' office?'

'Just up there.' He pointed to a small corridor on the left Tom hadn't noticed before.

'Can you see into the duty room from it?' Tom asked.

'No.'

'How long were you there?'

'Two or three minutes. I haven't been

much help, I'm afraid, but I thought it corroborated what Jane told you.'

'Yes, it does do that.' Tom made another note.

Sally said, 'Has Jane told you what she saw?'

'She has, yes.'

'Then surely, if Harry was doing anything with the computer, Jane would have seen him?'

Not if he'd sneaked round to your office to do it, she wouldn't ... 'I take your point,' he said.

The phone on the nurses' station rang and was answered by Katie, who'd reappeared.

'Children's Ward A, Student Nurse Ashfield ... Hold on please ... Sister, it's for you,' she called.

'Excuse me,' Sally said again, and walked over.

Jane said, 'If there's nothing more, Mr Jones, I'd better be getting on.'

'OK,' said Tom. 'Thanks for talking to me.'

As soon as she'd gone, Miller said quietly, 'Mr Jones, I wonder if I might have a word with you—' he glanced quickly over at Sally, who was still on the phone—'in private?'

'Your office?'

'No,' Miller said quickly, 'we might be

disturbed. D'you know the junior doctors' common room?'

'No.'

Sally put the phone down and started back towards them.

'Main corridor, left, about fifty yards,' he murmured. 'You can't miss it. I'd better be getting on myself,' he said in a louder voice as Sally rejoined them. She glanced at him, then turned to Tom.

'Is what you've heard any help?' She looked at him almost beseechingly.

Yes, but not in the way you were hoping. 'It certainly is important,' he said, 'and I think you should go to the police about it.'

'Thank you, Mr Jones, that's what I wanted to know.'

He felt slightly guilty for raising her hopes.

For once, *you can't miss it* proved to be the truth and ten minutes later, Tom let himself into the junior doctors' common room. Miller jumped up from where he was sitting and came over.

'Thanks for coming.' He led the way across the comfortable, sparsely inhabited room to a pair of armchairs in the corner. When Tom had sat down, Miller leaned forward and said quietly, 'Mr Jones, did Mr Benedict kill his son?'

'You must know that I can't answer that.'

'But he has been arrested and is being questioned about it?'

'Yes,' Tom said after a pause.

Miller gazed at him thoughtfully. 'I feel rather badly about what I'm doing now—telling tales out of school—but ... well, Mr Benedict's attitude to his son did rather puzzle me at the time. I put it down to awkwardness on his part then, but now, I'm not so sure.' He paused. 'He didn't hold the boy, or even touch him—he got the nanny to do everything.'

Tom said, 'You seem to be telling me that you think he did do it.'

'I'm telling you that he showed no sign of love or affection for the boy.'

Tom didn't say anything and Miller continued, 'As I said, I do feel badly about this because Sally, Sister Yate, is convinced he's a victim of injustice and was expecting me to back her up. She doesn't have much luck with men,' he added.

'How d'you mean?'

Miller smiled humourlessly. 'I mean, she don't 'alf pick 'em. You wouldn't think that anyone with her looks would have any problems that way, would you?' He slowly shook his head. 'You'd be wrong.'

'Why is that, d'you think?'

'I ... don't really know.' He hesitated, then continued, 'It could be because she thinks she can change people ... she does tend to pick men she thinks she can—' He broke off. 'Oh, I don't know, I'm probably talking nonsense.'

'You think that's why she picked Benedict, because she thought she could change him?'

'Very likely. Look, I didn't really ask you here to discuss Sally's love life.'

Tom, looking at the handsome face, said, 'Forgive my asking, but do you have some interest in that direction yourself?'

Again, Miller hesitated. 'She and I did have a relationship, yes, but it's over now. That's why I feel so badly about what I'm telling you.'

'I'm a little surprised, doctor. I'd have thought you were more her type—more than Mr Benedict, anyway.'

Miller said, 'We just didn't click at the time, and that's really all I want to say about it.'

'But you think that she's wrong about Benedict?'

'What I think, Mr Jones, is that Sally is capable of hiding her eyes from unpalatable truths, and that she'll grasp at any straw rather than face up to them.'

Tom decided to probe. 'Dr Miller, I can't help wondering whether there's some other reason you think Benedict might have killed his son, something you heard perhaps, something you—'

Miller's bleeper went and he smiled as he unclipped it from his pocket. 'I'm sorry, Mr Jones, but you really will have to excuse me now.'

23

Southey and Liz had a light lunch together, optimistic that things were going their way. By three o'clock, they weren't so sure.

Harry seemed to have mutated into a kind of insect, an utterly dispassionate insect with a thick, protective carapace. He displayed no feeling and answered every question in a flat, unemotional voice.

'Yes, I did know that Peter wasn't my natural son, but I loved him as though he were.'

'Then why did you pretend to us that you didn't know?' Liz asked.

'Because I felt ashamed of it.'

'What made you suspect that he wasn't your son?'

'After Tania was killed, I came to realise that he didn't look like me and wanted to know the truth. That's why I had the DNA test done.'

'Did you realise whose son he was?'

'Of course. Richard was the only other person it could have been.'

'He looked like Richard, then?'

'Not particularly.'

'You must have realised that Richard knew as well.'

'No. Why should he?'

'But he *did* know, didn't he? He challenged Tania about it.'

'So you say, but I didn't know that.'

'D'you really expect us to believe that?'

A shrug.

'What does that gesture mean, Mr Benedict? That shrug.'

'It means I don't know.' *Or care,* his expression seemed to add.

After a pause, Liz continued, 'You told us just now that you felt ashamed of the fact that Peter wasn't your natural son. The truth is, isn't it—' she leaned forward, as though sharing a confidence— 'that every time you looked at him, it was a reminder that Tania had been sleeping with Richard when you thought she'd been sleeping only with you. That you'd been cuckolded.'

A faint smile. 'As a matter of fact, it made me feel as though I had one over on him.'

271

'Oh, come on! You expect us to believe that?'

A shrug.

'What does that gesture mean, Mr Benedict?'

Harry didn't answer.

'The witness made no answer to my question.' Liz leaned forward again. 'And then you meet an attractive girl. You like her. Makes you feel like starting again. The trouble is, you've got a son. A son who isn't your son, a son who perhaps comes between you and your new girlfriend. Babysitters to organise every time you want to go out, always having to be back at a certain time. Constant interruptions, broken nights ...'

Harry shrugged.

'You realise that we know why you went back to the laboratory on Saturday?' They'd had another break and Southey had taken over the questioning. 'It was to cover your tracks, wasn't it? But what you *didn't* know was that Teresa had phoned Richard after you'd spoken to her and that he'd got there before you. That must have been a shock, especially when you realised he'd found out what you'd done. That's why you had to kill him, isn't it?'

'I killed him in self-defence because he attacked me.'

'I suppose, in a sense, that's true,' Southey mused. 'After all, he must have been pretty mad at you when he realised what you'd done. But a jury might suspect that Richard dead was a lot more use to you at that moment than Richard alive and talking. A tailor-made scapegoat, in fact.'

Harry shrugged.

'What does that gesture mean, Mr Benedict?'

Another break.

They probed from every angle they could think of, but he refused to be trapped, refused to react to anything they said. Then, at around seven, Larsen stood up.

'This has become a complete farce. You haven't been able to produce a single piece of solid evidence against my client, all you've succeeded in doing is reducing him to a persistent vegetative state. If you're going to insist on holding him, I'm going to insist on calling his doctor.'

Liz wanted to detain him overnight, but after some debate, Southey decided to let him go.

Tom was in the bath again when the phone went. He swore, pulled himself out, swore again as his ankle knocked painfully against the tap. He limped, dripping, over to the phone.

'Jones.'

'Tom, it's Liz ... have I caught you at a bad time?'

'No, no. I was only in the bath and whacked my ankle getting out.' He paused as she gave a peal of laughter. 'Is the name Kendall of German origin, or did you discover the delights of *schadenfreude* some other way?'

'I'm sorry, it was the way you said it. Listen, can I come and pick your brains? Liaise?'

'Only if we can do it in the bath.'

'I was thinking more of the hotel bar.'

'Where are you phoning from?'

'The hotel bar.'

'So history really does repeat itself,' he said, and then had to explain about Teresa. 'How did it go today?' he asked.

'That's what I want to talk to you about.'

'I'll be down in quarter of an hour.'

Some instinct had even made her choose the same table.

'What can I get you to drink?' Tom asked.

'Another one of these, please. Half a beer.'

He bought a pint for himself and took the drinks back to the table.

'Good news or bad?'

'We've had to release him.'

'Oh, *no.*'

'Yes, against my better judgement.' She told him about the three sessions they'd had with Harry.

'I thought you were looking tired,' he said quietly when she'd finished. 'You can't charge him with what you've got?'

'No.' She shook her head. 'In retrospect, we should have looked for more evidence before arresting him, but the super was so sure—' she gave a shamefaced smile— *'we,* I should say, we were so sure he'd break down when we faced him with it.'

'If it's any comfort, so was I.'

'We need at least one piece of solid evidence—someone who saw him using the computer at the right time, something to show why he went into the lab the following morning ... You still don't have any ideas about that?'

He shook his head. 'No, although not for lack of trying.' He told her how he'd been seeking inspiration from the sea when Sally had phoned him.

'It was as well you told us about that,' Liz said. 'I think the super would have thrown in the towel if you hadn't warned us that the staff nurse's story was flawed.' She paused. 'The sister claimed you told her that it would help Benedict.'

'I most certainly did not,' Tom said, 'I was very careful not to.' He paused. 'There was one other interesting thing, though. Dr

Miller—he's the house officer who was on duty when Peter was treated—arranged a rather cloak-and-dagger meeting with me after I'd seen Sister Sally.' He told her what Miller had said to him. 'I wanted to press him some more, but his bleeper went and he had to go.'

'D'you think he's holding back on something?'

'I'm not sure. It did occur to me he was jealous and simply wanted to do Benedict a bit of harm ... It wouldn't hurt for you to talk to him, though.'

'No.' She pulled a notebook out of her handbag. 'Miller, you said?'

He told her how to find him, then said, 'You could also try talking to Teresa Belling again.'

'I don't think there's any more we can get out of her, Tom.'

He said slowly, 'There was another thing we didn't follow up—Richard saying he would have liked to have brought Peter up himself. Teresa thought he was a bit obsessed, remember? I wonder if he'd done anything about it? It's something you could try on her.'

'I'll speak to her again tomorrow.' She made another note. 'What about the attack on Amina Khatoon, any more thoughts on that?'

'I'd almost forgotten it. I can't for the

life of me see how it fits in now.'

'No, neither can I. If you do think of anything, you will let me know, won't you?' She searched his face.

Tom smiled back at her. 'I seem to remember you suggesting that I'd become personally involved in this case—I can't help wondering if the same applies to you, now.'

'Perhaps it does,' she said in her slow, careful way. 'I'm sure we've got the right man—thanks to you—but if we can't find some more evidence, I've a horrible feeling he's going to get away with it. I wish we hadn't let him go tonight,' she added.

'What good would it have done, hanging on to him?'

'Oh, I don't know. I've just got this feeling he's going to give us the slip somehow.' She smiled wryly at him. 'Call it women's intuition, if you like.'

'I respect women's intuition,' he said.

She nodded, still smiling, and her presence, which until then had projected merely warmth, became suddenly electric. His body tingled with it.

She raised her glass, finished her drink. He said, 'Let me get you another.'

'Better not, I'm driving,' she said. 'I ought to be going soon, anyway.' But she didn't move.

Tom, looking at her almost classic

profile, heard himself say, 'Don't go.'

She looked up at him as he added, 'Stay here with me.' Even as he said it, he wasn't sure whether he really meant it.

She leaned over, kissed his cheek.

'We'd regret it, Tom. Please don't think I wouldn't like to, but sooner or later we'd regret it.'

On safe ground now, Tom said, 'But we wouldn't 'alf enjoy ourselves first.'

She stood up. 'Good-night, Tom.'

Her smile was like sunset. As she walked away, he realised that, although she'd turned him down, she'd been waiting, wanting him to ask, *needed* him to ask.

Aaaaah ... he thought as he watched her go. *Another time, perhaps. In another life.*

The next morning, she followed Tom's advice, which gave her enough information to arrest Harry again. But when they arrived at his house, Harry had gone.

24

So where did it all begin? Harry was wondering. *What exactly was the pivot of all the things that brought me here?*

Had it been when Tania first made

it clear she found him attractive? When she'd suggested they live together? Or was it when Peter had been conceived?

He glanced up at the rear-view mirror again to see if he was being followed. No, nothing ... He craned his neck, he couldn't help it, he *had* to look at his eyes again ... *Yes, that's what the eyes of a killer look like, a murderer—*

The horn blast of the oncoming car dropped an octave as it flashed past; Harry wrenched the wheel to pull the car back over to his own side of the road.

No, he thought, *not that way. But maybe that was the pivot, when Tania told me she wanted ...*

'It's not working, Harry,' she'd said as he drove out of the car-park and accelerated away. 'It was a mistake.' She'd been preoccupied throughout the meal and Harry's attempts to jolly her along had only resulted in a row.

'I'm sorry,' he said, 'I thought it might relax us.'

'I'm not talking about the meal, I'm talking about *us*, our relationship. It's not working.' She had been staring ahead; now, she took a breath and looked across at him. 'Why let it drag on when we can cut loose now with the minimum of pain?'

Harry couldn't believe what he was hearing—how had it degenerated into this? 'Are you saying you want us to split up?'

'Yes, Harry, I am. I'm sorry, but there's never a right time for this sort of thing, is there? I've been thinking about it for—'

'But what about Peter?' he managed, his voice sounding strange in his ears.

'What about him?'

'He's our son—whatever your, *our* feelings, we should at least make an effort for his sake.'

'It's a bit too late for that.'

He was still trying to think of a way of countering the terrible finality in her voice when she added, 'Besides, Harry ... he isn't your son.'

The instant she'd said it, he'd known it was true and something snapped in his mind. 'You bitch,' he'd said.

They'd been gaining on the lorry in front and he'd already begun pulling out. There was another car coming towards them, a shade close for comfort, but—

'Harry, what are you *doing?*' she screamed.

He put his foot down.

Or perhaps it had been when Richard had phoned just a fortnight before and asked if he could come round to his house to talk. Harry had been surprised then, but that was nothing compared to the way he'd felt once Richard had started ...

'This feud between us, it's gone on long enough.'

Harry shrugged. 'No arguments there.'

'We both know what's at the bottom of it. If we can sort that out, we can get on with our lives.'

Harry waited.

'Peter's my son. Born out of wedlock, but conceived in love, and my son. I want to give him a proper home. I want him back.'

'*Y'what?*' Harry jerked as if electrocuted.

'I want my son back. We can arrange it in a civilised manner and—'

'You must be out of your fuckin' bovine mind.' Harry had jumped to his feet. 'Get out! Get out of my house.'

Richard slowly stood up. 'I was hoping we could be civilised about this, but if you won't co-operate, I shall apply through the courts for a residence order, which as his natural father, I shall get.'

'Bollocks, he's lived with me since he was born, that's the status quo and that's the way it's staying.'

Richard shook his head. 'I've done my homework.' He smiled, took some sheets of paper from his pocket and dropped them on the table. 'If you'd married Tania, even on the day before she'd died it *would*

281

have given you custody. But you didn't, and that's why I shall get it.'

The sheets were photocopies from a law book that showed that Richard might, in fact, have a case.

'Oh, what the fuck does it matter where the pivot was?' he muttered aloud. 'They're all dead ...' *and I'm responsible,* he thought. *I killed them. Tania. Peter. Richard. And now me, a dead man driving ...*

A quarter of an hour later, he parked the car and set off on foot. Twenty minutes after that, he reached his destination.

I'm the most powerful man in the world, he thought, *I've got absolutely nothing left to lose. I can do whatever I like ...* He opened the bottle he'd brought with him, took a deep swig and lit a nail.

It was after midday by the time Liz phoned Tom and told him what had happened.

'You were right,' she said. 'Kelso had been to his solicitor about claiming custody of Peter—apparently, he stood a chance of getting it.'

'Ah ...'

'The thing is,' she continued, 'we think Benedict might be intending to top himself. D'you have any idea where he might have gone?'

'No,' Tom said slowly, 'I'm afraid I don't.'

'Can you think of anyone who might?'

'I suppose Sister Sally would be the best bet.'

'We've tried her.'

'Teresa?'

'Her too.'

'The only other possibility is Amina.'

'Yes ... she'll be out of hospital by now, won't she?'

'D'you know her address?'

'I don't, offhand. Sorry.'

'It's all right, I'll find it. Thanks, Tom.' She rang off.

Poor Amina ... he thought.

He had a sandwich at the bar, then went out for some cheroots. After that, he made his way over to the pier again. Sea, sun and air were all as they'd been the day before. He smoked a cheroot, chatted with a fisherman, leaned against the rail looking out to sea ... and then his mobile phone rang.

'Oh, bloody hell!' he said aloud, attracting more stares than the phone had done. He extracted it, extended the aerial and shouted, 'Hang *on* a minute.'

He looked round. A little way back down the pier was a wooden shack and he went and crouched in its lee. 'Hello?'

'Tom, it's me. Holly.'

'Holly?'

'Your wife, remember? Where are you that makes it so difficult to talk?'

'In a force five on the end of Regis pier.'

'What are you doing there?'

'Trying to relax. You know, get away from it all.'

She gave a rich chuckle.

'Anyway, to what do I owe the pleasure ...?'

Her tone immediately became more serious. 'I've had Amina Khatoon on the phone to me.'

'Amina? How did she get our number?'

'She rang my parents, who rang and gave me hers. She wants to see you.'

'Did she say why?'

'It's about Harry Benedict, that's all she'd say. But she said she wouldn't tell you anything unless you promised not to tell the police.'

'Holly, you know I can't do that.'

'Go and talk to her, Tom, she sounded absolutely desperate. If you're straight with her, she'll tell you.'

'Did she say where she was?'

'At home. I've got her address here.'

Tom took it down, said goodbye and walked back to his car. He looked up the address in the street map, wondered whether he should ring Liz ... No, best to go and see Amina, see what he could find out and then no nonsense about Boy Scout's honour.

She lived in a neat terrace about a mile from the hospital. The door was freshly painted and the small front garden overflowed with late summer flowers, somehow as exotic as herself. The door opened almost as soon as he rang.

'Come in, Mr Jones.' As though to confound him, she was dressed in blouse and jeans.

She closed the door behind him, silently led him to an intimate, entirely feminine living-room.

'Do please sit down.' She sat down herself, regarded him. The swelling on her lip had gone and her hair was tied up with a scarf, presumably to hide a bandage.

'Are you feeling better?' he asked.

'Thank you, yes.' She seemed more fragile than ever, holding herself in tight control. She said, 'Did your wife explain the position to you?'

'Yes.'

'Do I have your word that you won't go to the police?'

'That has to depend on what you tell me,' he hedged. 'You must see that.'

'It isn't good enough.'

'Amina, the police think he might be

going to kill himself.'

'I know. I think that too.'

'Then wouldn't it be better if you told me?'

She leaned forward. 'Mr Jones, I can persuade him to give himself up.'

'How? Why would he listen to you?'

'He will. Wouldn't it be better that way?'

'Of course it would, but he's killed two people already. He's dangerous, you could end up getting killed yourself.'

'That won't happen.'

'How can you know that?'

'I just know.'

He wasn't going to get any more. 'All right, you have my word,' he said, mentally crossing his fingers. 'D'you know where he is?'

She stared back at him, hesitating. 'I think I know where he might be.'

Sister Sally was right, he thought, *she is like a frightened deer* ... 'Where?'

She said, 'He may have killed Richard, in self-defence, but he didn't kill Peter.'

'How do you know that?'

'I just know,' she said again.

Tom gazed back at her—was it blind faith, or was there something else she knew?

'What do you want me to do?' he said.

She leaned forward again. 'Take me

to him. Let me persuade him to give himself up.'

'You'll have to tell me where he is.'

'I'll give you directions as we drive.'

'All right.' *I'll use the mobile when we get there—damn, she's bound to notice it before then ...*

'Shall we go?' she said, getting up. He followed her into the hall. She took a jacket from the stand, then opened the door to let him out.

He unlocked the car, got in and leaned over to unlock her door, palming and hiding the mobile under the seat as he did.

'Which way?' he said as she got in.

'D'you know the way to Wareham?'

'I can find it.' The old music hall joke flitted through his mind: *Is this the way to Wareham? No, you've got 'em on back to front ...*

He reached for the road atlas, found the page. 'Perhaps you'd like to navigate,' he said, proffering it to her.

She looked at him as though suspecting a trap, then took it. 'All right.'

He started the car.

'Left at the end of the road,' she said.

They drove down to the seafront and out of town. There wasn't much traffic and he let the Cooper go along the straight by the sea-wall, the exhaust echoing from it to be lost in the reeds of the salt-marsh on the other side. He slowed as they came to a built-up area.

'Which way?' he enquired.

'Just follow the road. I'll tell you when you need to turn.'

After the village the road wound tortuously up. The sea below sparkled briefly, then went out of sight as they turned inland. They came to a roundabout built round a clump of Scots Pine.

'Go right here,' she said.

He drove fast along a dual carriageway. She was looking uneasy, but he didn't think it was the speed. *We're getting warmer,* he thought.

The dual carriageway ended and the countryside flattened, as though somebody had pulled it straight, like a tablecloth. A couple of miles later, she said suddenly, 'Take the next turning on the right.'

They were almost on it and he had to brake and swerve to get round.

A village almost unnatural in its prettiness ... 'Keep going,' she said.

The road narrowed, twisted down, slid into a shallow valley. They drove in silence for about five minutes, then she said, 'Go right here.'

The signpost said 'Durdle Door' ...

Durdle Door, where had he heard of that before? Ah, a caravan park, so he was hiding in a caravan ...

'Keep going,' she said. Her voice was trembling. They passed a lodge with a sign marked 'Reception'.

'In here,' she said, and he turned right, into a field. 'Over there.' She pointed to a car in the corner, a blue Escort, Harry's car.

He parked beside it. It was empty.

'Now what?' he said.

'You wait here. You gave me your word, remember?'

'How long will you be?'

Her tongue touched her lips. 'I don't know.' She pushed the door open. 'Don't follow me.'

She closed the door, walked past Harry's car, climbed over a stile and on to a path. As soon as her head sank from view, Tom felt under her seat for the mobile.

Shit! She'd found it and taken it with her.

He started the car and drove quickly back to the lodge. A bored-looking youth sat behind the counter.

'Is there a phone I could use, please?'

The boy pointed to a booth in the corner. Tom found some change, dialled.

'Inspector Kendall, please ... Tell her it's Tom Jones.' He fidgeted as he waited to be put through.

'Liz, it's Tom. I'm at Durdle Door with

Amina Khatoon. Benedict's car's here, empty. She's gone down to look for him, I'm about to follow.'

'Tom—'

He disconnected before she could say any more, said 'Thanks' to the boy and started back out.

'It's two pounds if you're using the car-park,' the boy said.

Tom found some coins and slapped them on the counter. He drove back, jumped over the stile and followed the path down. It was well worn, very stony. It turned right and descended steeply down the side of the slope. A figure at the bottom disappeared—Amina.

He began running, lengthening his stride and allowing gravity to pull him faster and faster as he concentrated on avoiding the stones. He'd almost reached the bottom when his foot slid on a pebble and he found himself flying ... he put out his hands, described an almost perfect cartwheel before landing *crump* like a stack of paper. He lay there a moment, heaved in a few breaths, then picked himself up and realised where he'd heard of Durdle Door before.

The land below had been eroded behind the cliff face so that a section of it stood out to sea like a hammer-head. The right-hand promontory had an enormous hole punched in it, almost perfectly the shape of a barn door. White-capped waves surged through and on to the shingle beach behind.

Durdle Door, where Sergeant Troy had pretended to commit suicide in Thomas Hardy's *Far From the Madding Crowd*.

But is that what Benedict's doing? He pulled his eyes away and looked for Amina ... there she was, at the foot of the hammerhead. As though by telepathy, she glanced back, saw him and started climbing the steep grassy slope. Tom found a flight of steps, went down as fast as he could, ducked under a wire fence and started after her. His shoe slipped on some mud and he fell to his knees ... righted himself and went on, willing his legs to push harder. His thighs ached, his breath grew ragged ...

Amina had tired too, her breath coming in anguished sobs. She glanced back, saw Tom ten yards below her and gritted her teeth for a final effort. She'd nearly reached the top when his hand went round her ankle—she tried to kick, but with a tiny scream, fell back into his arms.

The weight of her broke his own foothold and they fell, scrabbling desperately as they slithered down. The sea below them beckoned briefly, then Tom's foot found a purchase and they stopped.

Amina was utterly spent. All she could

do was gasp, 'You promised, you *promised* ...'

As soon as Tom could speak, he said, 'Amina, he could kill you, I couldn't risk that.' He heaved in a breath. 'Where is he?'

'... told you ... he won't harm me ...'

'Why, Amina?' He had to get it out of her now. 'What is it you know? *Why* won't he harm you?'

Her eyes twisted round. 'Because I'm pregnant ... I'm carrying his child.'

25

It was true, had to be, and it explained ... but *what* did it explain?

'Does he know?'

'No. Please let me tell him, Mr Jones, it might make a difference.' A bead of sweat found its way into her eye and she blinked it away.

'How?'

'It—it might give him something to live for.'

'He's not that kind of person, Amina.'

'Please let me try.'

Tom hesitated. 'Where is he, exactly?'

'There's a sort of ledge on the other side,

his eyrie, he calls it. He comes here when he wants to think.'

Tom looked up. 'Just on the other side?'

'No, a little way to the right and down. Please, Mr Jones.'

It could be half an hour before the police came, and their arrival would probably make it even less likely he'd give himself up ...

'All right,' he said, 'I'll give you ten minutes. After that ...' After that, what?

To his surprise, she quickly kissed his cheek, then turned and started back up. A few moments later, she was over the top.

He waited a minute, then started climbing himself. Now that he wasn't chasing anyone, it was a lot easier.

Abruptly, the slope flattened and the wind tugged at his hair and ears. The top was narrower than he'd expected, not much more than a wide ridge. He crawled over it, peered down the other side. A steep grassy slope dotted with yellow flowers fell away into air; below, a chain of rocks like rotted teeth stood out of the ruffled sea. He caught a snatch of talk on the wind, Amina's voice. Keeping as low as he could, he crawled along the ridge towards it.

Harry had finished the whisky, but he wasn't drunk, not really drunk, not the way he wanted to be—oh, why hadn't he brought another bottle, more nails? Even the sea had let him down ...

Well, what did you expect, jerker? A revelation, a starburst of truth ...?

The ledge was about five feet by eight, thirty feet above the water. He'd come to watch the sea catch fire, the way it had when he was here with Tania ... 'Look, Harry,' she'd said, 'if you half close your eyes, it looks like there's a fire on the bottom of the sea.'

It had, too; had again after she'd died, but not today. The sea had been his friend then, but he wasn't sure that it was any more.

He shivered; it was chilly in the wind, despite the whisky. *I can't even get this right,* he thought. *I'm a total, fucking failure.* His throat closed, then his eyes and before he knew it he was weeping again.

'Harry?'

He slowly turned his face, expecting to see Tania.

'I thought you were afraid of heights,' he said when he saw who it was. In his disappointment, it was all he could think of to say.

'I wanted to see you.'

'Why?'

She hesitated. A down-draught of wind blew hair over her face and she pushed it away. 'To tell you that I'm pregnant.'

He gave a harsh bark of laughter. 'You poor thing.'

'I'm glad, Harry.'

'Why, for God's sake? You want a murderer's child?'

'I know you're not a murderer.'

'I am.' He turned away, and now the drink did take hold of him. He began muttering: 'They're all dead—Tania, Peter, Richard. And now Harry ...' His lips moved.

'Come back with me, Harry. Please. We'll get it sorted, I promise.'

He shook his head, peering down at the sea. 'No.'

'Harry—'

'How did you get here?' he demanded suddenly. He pushed himself on to his feet, stumbled over to her. 'You haven't got a car.'

'A taxi,' she said quickly.

'I don't believe you.' He grabbed her wrist. 'Who brought you here? The police?'

'A—a friend. Harry, you're hurting me ...'

'What friend?' He swayed in the wind for a moment, staring at her, then clambered a little way up from the ledge.

'Well, well, if it isn't Mr Dogshit Jones. Well, you can fuck off back where you came from, Dogshit.'

Tom slowly got to his feet. Harry jumped back on to the ledge and grabbed Amina by the shoulders. 'Fuck off, or she goes over.'

He won't, Tom thought. *But then again, he might ... If I'm honest,* he thought, *something like this was inevitable.*

Harry and Amina stood unmoving as though part of a tableau, then Harry said suddenly, 'Got any nails on you, Dogshit?'

'Cheroots any good?'

'Sure. Toss 'em over.'

Tom brought the packet out from his pocket. *Jump him as he goes to pick them up ...?* He opened the pack. 'One for myself,' he said, putting it between his lips. He came forward, tossed the pack down.

'Thanks,' Harry said. 'Now, piss off.'

Tom said, 'Let Amina come with me.'

'D'you want to go with him, Amina?'

She shook her head.

'She doesn't want to go with you.'

Tom said, 'Give yourself up, Harry. The police'll be here soon.'

'I don't remember asking you to call me Harry ... Anyway, why should I give myself up?' he sneered.

'For Amina's sake. For the baby's.'

Harry felt anger building inside him—a familiar, sustaining anger. 'You know a hell of a lot about me, don't you, Dogshit?

Anything you don't know?'

'Quite a bit, I expect.' *Divert his attention on to me?* 'I do know how you killed Peter, and why. And that Richard attacked you that morning because he'd found out.'

Harry felt his skin burning, as though with static electricity; his fingertips, his eyelids crackled with it as it tried to force its way out of his body. 'I've changed my mind, Dogshit,' he said. 'Come and join us.'

Amina, recognising the tone deep in his voice, said, 'Go away, Mr Jones. Please ...'

Harry shifted her sideways and she stumbled a foot nearer the edge. 'Down here, *now.*'

Tom lowered himself down, jumped the last few feet. The ledge was covered in sea pink, springy under his feet.

Harry said, 'I suppose it was you who worked it all out and told the police.'

'That's right.'

Another filament inside Harry's head snapped. He pushed Amina aside and lunged at Tom, taking him completely by surprise. His fingers clamped Tom's arms and Tom had time only to think, *God, he's strong,* as Harry twisted him round and forced him backwards to the edge ...

'Harry, *no* ...' Amina screamed. She

caught one of his arms and tried to pull him back.

Harry wrenched it free and gave her a shove that sent her sprawling. Tom punched at his head with his free hand, then, as Harry let go the other in surprise, wrapped both arms round Harry's midriff and, grunting with the effort, started pushing him back from the edge.

Harry flailed his exposed shoulders, and when that didn't do any good, jerked his knee up into Tom's face.

Tom relaxed his hold enough for Harry to wrench his arms away. Harry heaved and Tom staggered back ... Harry ran at him, shoved again ... Tom windmilled briefly, then toppled backwards over the edge ...

Amina, who'd been dazed by the fall, screamed again. Harry looked round at her, his face puzzled, then back to where Tom had been. He blinked, then, giving himself room, he ran, jumping as far out from the ledge as he could ...

Tom squirmed in the air in a vain effort to control his fall, saw all the myriad images he'd always supposed he'd see, and it seemed to take a lot longer than a second to fall thirty feet, but then the sea reached up for him.

The water broke most of his fall, but his head struck a rock a few feet under and he didn't even feel the cold.

Harry rolled himself into a ball, then he, too, hit the water. He felt his back strike something hard, then the cold hit him. Instinctively, he pushed down with his feet, broke surface.

He was surrounded by spume and weed-strewn rocks; the cliff face reared above him. There was no sign of Jones.

Well, this is what you wanted, isn't it, to be among friends ... Then his legs bumped into something that wasn't rock and he grabbed at it.

Clothes ... He pulled, and Tom's head came dripping out of the water, his mouth hanging open. A wave pushed them toward the cliff, just a few feet away. He got his arm round Tom's neck, kicked backwards as he tried to swim away from the rocks, thinking, *If I can just get to the door* ...

His back bumped into something hard, he worked down with his feet, trying to manoeuvre round it ... Limpets gouged his arm and shoulder but he hardly felt them ... Waves slapped his face, an undertow from the cliff pulled him down. He thrust his feet against the rock, gained a yard and then saw a sliver of light ... the door!

It must be twenty bloody feet away, I'll never ... His clothes dragged on his body ... Another wave submerged Tom's face, then his own ... He spat water, heaved a salt-filled breath, knew he couldn't make it ...

But it's what you wanted, you can't complain.

They were sucked under again: he threshed vainly, then a foot found a purchase and he heaved upwards. He lifted his head—the door, he'd nearly reached it! The current must have taken them along the cliff face.

So the sea had relented ... He thrust a foot sideways to clear the rocks at the door's edge, then tried to force his legs into a frog stroke, allowing the friendly waves to push him through. His limbs were feebly waving tendrils and he couldn't feel a thing, not the cold, not his limbs, not even the salty slaps of the waves. He looked down at Tom's face, thought, *He's probably dead anyway, why am I bothering?*

He dragged another breath, looked over his shoulder and laughed, or would have done if he'd had the strength. Two policemen were wading into the water to help him.

Tom and Liz were in a dell beside a stream and she tilted her face and kissed him. He slid his tongue into her mouth, her own responded and everything became possible ...

Then, in quite another voice. she said,

'Well, there's nothing much wrong with you.'

He opened his eyes. '*No ...*' he groaned, 'I want to go back.'

She looked down at him, puzzled. 'Back where, Tom?'

Ten minutes later, he'd recovered enough to hobble slowly up the path, a police jacket round his shoulders. He shivered uncontrollably, he was dizzy and his head throbbed exquisitely. They'd phoned for ambulances from the beach, and they were waiting for them at the top. Harry went handcuffed and with police escort. Amina insisted on going with him.

Liz took the call as they were coming back into Regis and directed the driver to the nurses' home. Another police car and a van were already there.

She was taken to the room. A body lay face down on the bed and the police photographer was lining up his camera for another angle.

'Is it her?' Liz asked. *Or should that be she?* she wondered irrelevantly. She'd never got used to death.

'Yeah, that's Katie Ashfield.' The officer pointed to the name badge on the uniform hanging over the chair. 'You'd better have a look at this.'

He showed her the portable typewriter

on the desk against the wall. A sheet of paper protruded from the roller.

Dear Mum
I'm sorry, but it's best this way. I killed a baby. I didn't mean to, I only wanted to give his father a scare because he was so rude. I really didn't think he'd die. Sorry, Mum—I love you. Katie.

So this is where it ends, Liz thought, looking round the room, then back at Katie's mortal remains. *How squalid,* she thought, *or do I mean meaningless ...?*

'That window,' she said to the officer. 'Was it open when you came in?'

'Yeah. We didn't touch anything, other than the door.'

A noise behind them announced the arrival of the police doctor.

Tom opened his eyes to find Liz sitting by his bed.

'Have you come to kiss me again?' he enquired.

'Certainly not.' She smiled to take the sting out of it. 'That was in the line of duty.' Then she said, 'What did you mean when you said you wanted to go back?'

He tried to think. 'All I can remember is that we were in a place where only you and I existed, and we were ...' He

302

tailed off, shrugged and grinned back at her.

'Well,' she said after a pause, 'we'll just have to think about the other Tom and Liz having a nice time there, won't we?' Her own smile faded slightly. 'How are you feeling?'

'Not too bad. Head still aches.'

'D'you feel up to talking?'

'I suppose you want to know why I went off with Amina without telling you?'

'No, she's already explained about that. There's been another development.'

'Benedict's confessed?'

'He has, as a matter of fact, but the doctors say he'd confess to being Spring-Heeled Jack in his present state. He's a real mess, you know, ridden with guilt, and they're saying he'll need months of psychotherapy ... but that wasn't the development I meant.'

'Well, what *is* it?'

'While you were having your swim, we—some of my colleagues, that is—were looking for a nurse from the Children's Ward who'd been reported missing.'

'Which nurse?'

'Katie Ashfield—d'you know her?'

'I do, yes. Have they found her?'

'They have.' Her face lost all trace of humour. 'Dead. In her room at the nurses' home, apparently of a drug overdose. She left a note, confessing to the murder of Peter Benedict.'

'Bloody hell!' Then, 'Is it true, d'you think?'

'It's quite possible, since no one seems to know exactly where she was at the time.'

'What did the note say?'

Liz found her notebook and read it out.

'Signed?' Tom asked.

'No, it was still in the typewriter. We do get them like that.'

'Mm. Tell me everything, the lot—from the moment you got there.'

She did so.

'So what are you doing about Benedict?' he asked some time later. 'Are you releasing him?'

'Not yet, there's still a lot more checking to do, not least a PM on the nurse. But it isn't looking quite so black for him now.'

'I did wonder why he went to so much bother to fish me out of the briny,' Tom mused.

Then the door opened and Holly and Marcus came in. Holly was carrying Hal, who croaked a greeting as he saw his father.

Liz Kendall smiled and quietly withdrew.

'Hal, *no!*'

It was an hour later and Marcus had

left Tom with Holly and Hal. Holly picked up the leaflets Hal had knocked from the bedside cabinet and began replacing them in their plastic holder.

'They do pretty well down here for culture,' she commented, looking at one of them. 'The Bournemouth Symphony Orchestra, no less. I'd have rather liked to have gone to this.'

'What are they playing?'

'*Were* playing—it was a week ago. Mozart and Haydn. The 'Surprise' Symphony and the twenty-ninth—K201.'

'Can I see that a moment, please?' Tom said after a pause.

Holly passed it to him and he thoughtfully studied it.

26

There was a light tap on the door, then Sally put her head round. 'Can I come in?'

'Please do,' said Tom, putting his newspaper down. 'Come and have a seat.' He indicated the chair next to his bedside cabinet.

It was late the next day and, due to complications, Tom was still in bed, still in the same room. Sally sat down and carefully crossed her legs. She was wearing her uniform.

'So how are you feeling?' she asked.

'Pretty good, considering,' Tom replied. 'Thanks.'

'Thanks for your message,' she said. 'I'd wondered about coming to see you earlier, but I wasn't sure whether you'd want any visitors. Anyway, I'm glad for the opportunity to say thank you—from Harry and me.'

Tom chuckled. 'I'm not sure I deserve any thanks, from Harry anyway. Have you seen him?'

Her brow creased. 'Yesterday, and then only briefly—he's still under arrest. Why *is* that, Mr Jones? Surely the police accept that he didn't do it now?'

'Well, there is the fact that he tried to run away, and there is still the matter of Richard Kelso outstanding.'

'Yes, I suppose so.'

'When did you first suspect that Nurse Ashfield might have been responsible for Peter's death?' Tom asked.

'I'm not sure that I did, not until I heard about the confession she'd left. I just knew there was something odd about her.'

'When did you realise she was missing?'

'Oh, not until yesterday morning, when she didn't turn up for duty.'

'It was as well you realised that she might be suicidal and got on to the police so quickly.'

'Instinct, perhaps.' She gave a wry smile. 'We're trained to be on the look-out for odd behaviour these days. Sign of the times, I'm afraid.'

'And it was certainly fortuitous for Harry that she decided to bring things to a conclusion at this time.'

'Oh, I don't know. Harry's arrest must have concentrated her mind.'

'Yes. Curious, though, that neither Peter's nor Richard Kelso's death had the same concentrating power.'

She looked askance at him. 'What do you mean, Mr Jones? I don't follow you.'

'Just thinking aloud.' He smiled. 'I've had a lot of time for thinking, cooped up in here, so I've been casting my mind back over the case.'

'Oh?'

'Yes. When I first got here, nearly a week ago now, I assumed, along with everyone else, that Richard Kelso must have killed Peter—partly because of the strength of his motive, and partly because of the narrowness of the window of opportunity. D'you understand what I mean by that?'

'I think so—because there was no time for anyone else to have done it.'

'Exactly. But later, after I'd looked at

the way the computer system works here, I realised that other people in the lab could have done it. And then, later still, when I thought Harry was responsible, I realised that it could have been someone on the ward. Now, of course, we have Nurse Ashfield's confession; but in fact, it could have been done by *anyone* on the ward. Dr Miller, Staff Nurse Radford. Even you could have done it.'

She gave a peal of silvery laughter. 'How perfectly ridiculous. What possible reason could any of us have for doing such a thing?'

'Well, Dr Miller might have been jealous of Harry—he did tell me all about his—er—past relationship with you.'

'How very gall*ant* of him,' she said drily, stressing the second syllable.

'He also told me about your ... difficulties with men in the past.'

'The only reason I've had difficulties with men, as you put it, is because so many men are like him.'

'But you are very fond of Harry, aren't you? I mean, you *want* Harry very much?'

'I've never made any secret of that. It's what makes your suggestion so ridiculous.'

'What suggestion?'

'That I'd harm Peter.'

'Did I say that?'

'Yes, you did, in so many words. I'd

never have done anything to harm Peter.'

'You might, if you thought he was in the way.'

She laughed again. 'I don't believe I'm hearing this—how could a one-year-old boy be in my way?'

'Well, he was always *there*, wasn't he? Sometimes in the background, sometimes in the foreground, but always there. Everything you and Harry did had to be planned around him, because, for all his faults, Harry wouldn't neglect his own son, his own flesh and blood.'

'But he wasn't his own ...'

'Yes?'

She took a deep breath. 'Peter wasn't his own son,' she said evenly. 'As I'm sure you already know.'

'Yes, but how did *you* know?'

She considered him afresh with narrowed eyes, then said, 'I found the result from the DNA lab in his desk, at his home.' She smiled. 'Yes, Mr Jones, I was being nosy. But you're right, of course, Harry wouldn't have neglected Peter anyway. It was one of the reasons I admired him so much.'

'So you say. The fact is, though, that Harry had begun to wonder about you and was looking for an excuse to get shot of you.'

She stared at him. 'What absolute rubbish!'

'No. You see, my mistake was to think that Harry killed Peter because he was worried about losing you, whereas in fact, he was worried because he didn't want Peter on your ward when he dumped you.'

'No—'

'Just as all the men in your life have wondered about you and dumped you.'

She swallowed, drew in another breath. 'I really don't understand what you mean, other than the fact that you're being very rude to me.'

'I mean that you've never been able to hold on to any man, despite your looks. As soon as they begin to realise what you're really like, they back off, don't they?' He regarded her. 'Why is that, d'you think? Münchhausen's Syndrome by proxy, that'd be my guess.'

Her mouth tightened into a tight, pinched prune; it was as though a screen had fallen away and another person entirely was looking at him from her face, then her features relaxed again and she said evenly, 'I haven't found the right person yet, it's true. Until now, that is—I have now, in Harry.'

Tom slowly shook his head. 'No. Harry was going to dump you, and inside, you knew it—'

'*No!*'

'—and you told yourself that it was

because of Peter. If it wasn't for Peter, you thought to yourself, things would work out this time. That's what you told yourself, isn't it?'

'This is ridiculous,' she said again. 'How could Peter's death possibly benefit me? This is—'

'Because you would have had Harry all to yourself, and because, in his shocked state, he would have become dependent on you. Or so you thought.'

She stared at him open-mouthed. 'You must have the most extraordinary imagination. It's completely irrelevant anyway—I couldn't have done it, I wasn't there.'

'But you *were* there, in your office at your computer terminal, altering Peter's lab result.'

'But that was *Katie*, I was—'

'No. You came back to the ward *before* Katie went to look for you. You heard her telling Harry that the lab was on the phone, then ducked into your office without anyone seeing you. It would have taken you less than half a minute to change that—'

'But we know that it was Katie in my office.' She'd regained her composure now, and was speaking calmly and confidently. 'The police have her confession.'

'Typed and unsigned—anyone could have done it.'

'Are you suggesting that I killed her as well?'

'I know damn well you did.'

'Oh, this really is the limit. How could I have possibly done that?'

'It would have been a lot easier for you to have got hold of Nitrazepam than for Katie.'

'We don't keep Nitrazepam capsules on the Children's Ward.'

'That's interesting. How did you know it was capsules?'

She hesitated, then said, 'Because Nitrazepam is more commonly available in capsule form.'

'But you did visit ITU the day before yesterday and borrow the key to the emergency drug store there, didn't you?'

'Yes, to get some Dihydrocodeine.'

'I know you did. But there are also some Nitrazepam capsules missing.'

'Well, I can't help that. Anyway—' she gave a quick, quirky smile— 'It's not possible to force someone to take capsules against their will.'

'It is if you chloroform them first.' He smiled back at her, then said, 'The only thing I don't know, sister, is whether you killed Katie just to provide a scapegoat, or whether she saw you coming out of your office when she came back from Ward B. Which was it? Was she blackmailing you?'

Sally had jumped to her feet and now a third person was staring down at him from her face. 'That, Mr Jones, is something you will never know ...'

Something in his own face, some satisfaction, made her pause, and then yet another personality blazed from her eyes, a force so malignant that he found himself shrinking away from her.

Then all the screens fell back into place and she was Sally again, saying loudly and clearly, 'And you will never know because it didn't happen. I can see no point in prolonging this conversation.'

She left the room, gently pulling the door to, then went quickly back through the corridors to Children's Ward A. No one tried to stop her. In her office, she looked up a number, picked up the phone and keyed it in.

'Ford and Squires, solicitors, can we help you?'

'Could I speak to Mr Squires, please ... Mr Squires? It's Sister Sally Yate here ... I'm fine, thanks, and you? ... Good. Listen, something quite extraordinary has just happened and I may need your help ...'

Tom was saying to Southey and Liz Kendall, 'Well, do you believe me now?'

'Yes,' Southey said. 'But even if that

313

were admissible as evidence—' he pointed to the tape— 'it wouldn't be anything like enough.'

'But the point is, you now *know,* and knowing, you should be able to find enough evidence.'

'She's forewarned, of course,' said Liz.

'That was inevitable,' Tom said. 'But I did leave most of your surprises intact.'

Liz smiled. 'It *was* observant of you to spot how she'd known Richard Kelso's password.' She pointed to the concert programme. 'K201.'

Southey had had a talk with Harry, who'd confirmed that Sally was adept with computers, and that he'd told her about Richard's password, including the BITCH part of it, when she'd shown him the music programme. Afterwards, he'd asked Southey not to allow Sally to visit him any more.

'It was luck,' Tom said modestly, omitting to mention Holly's part in it. 'And once I'd seen that, everything else flowed into place. She was good with computers, knew Richard's password and had the opportunity for both killings. She was obsessive, jealous and psychotic. It was highly unlikely that Katie Ashfield would have known Richard's password; on the other hand, she might have seen Sally coming out of her office, which would have made her doubly expendable. Add to that the preliminary forensic evidence that Katie probably didn't kill herself, and that Sally could easily have got hold of the Nitrazepam ...' He shrugged his shoulders nonchalantly, but still managed to look smug.

It hadn't been easy persuading Southey to the subterfuge with Sally, but once Tom had shown him the possibilities, plus the probability that Sally would be more than a match for conventional police questioning, he'd allowed it to go ahead.

'I'll tell you the worst bit,' Tom said now. 'It was just after she told me that whether Katie had been blackmailing her or not was something I'd never know, remember? She realised at that point I was wired, and something extremely nasty looked out of her eyes—I really thought she was going to go for me. I tell you, it terrified me. No wonder the men back off when they sense it.'

'Well, I think you're a Superhero,' Liz said, straight-faced.

Tom sniffed. He knew he'd never be able to describe properly the evil he'd seen at that moment.

'The inspector's a hard woman,' he complained to Southey.

'On the contrary,' said Southey, who knew perfectly well how Tom felt about her, 'she's a valued and right-thinking police officer. Just as you're a respectable married man.'

Once the possible significance of the open window in Katie's room had been appreciated, the pathologist had looked for, and found, traces of chloroform in Katie's lungs. He also found the bruising on her arms where she'd been held while the chloroform pad was applied, and the lesions in her throat where the capsules had been forced down while she was unconscious. And best of all, Sally had actually been seen going into the nurses' home the evening before, and was still unaware of the fact.

'More evidence would be nice,' Southey said, 'but I think she'll confess when we hit her with what we've got.'

Sally didn't confess at first, but then more forensic evidence was found (scrapings of skin under Katie's fingernails, fibres from Sally in Katie's room) and she was persuaded to admit to the killings and plead diminished responsibility.

Ironically, she'd never have been convicted of Peter's murder if she hadn't confessed to it, and she'd only murdered Katie in an attempt to save Harry.

She also admitted to the attacks on Amina. Realising, in the canteen, that

Harry was still fond of her, she had also recognized Amina's pregnancy and confirmed it by finding her medical notes in the computer.

Tom and Holly were driving away from Harry and Amina's wedding.

'It won't last,' Tom said. 'Benedict may be an unlucky bastard, but he's still a bastard.'

'Oh, that's rather hard, Tom,' said Holly. 'He had a lousy childhood, what with an alcoholic mother and no father. He's weak, oversexed and sexually attractive, which is a pretty lethal combination, and he fell in with some very egotistical women.'

'Mm,' said Tom.

'It's strange,' she mused, 'how all three of them—Harry, Tania and Sister Yate, I mean—came unstuck searching for the perfect partner.'

'Mm,' said Tom again, wondering how much she'd guessed about his feelings for Liz.

'Besides,' Holly continued, 'I think you may be underestimating Amina's strength of character.'

'Ah, the reforming power of a good woman,' Tom said, relieved to be off the subject of perfect partners. 'Not very PC though, is it, that?'

'Oh, I don't know,' Holly said airily.

'Harry still hasn't found a job, you know,' —he'd been found guilty of Richard's manslaughter and given a suspended sentence— 'and she'll get her Master's degree easily enough now she's taken over his PCR work. Once she's had the baby, she'll be eminently more employable than him.' She frowned. 'Or should that be he? Anyway, it'll make sense for him to be the one who stays at home.'

Tom chuckled, 'Harry's Nemesis. He'll be PC, because of PCR.'

Harry and Amina were also driving away. He put his hand out and squeezed her knee.

'Glad it's over?'

'Oh, yes and no. It was nice seeing all those people.'

'How're you feeling?'

'Tired, but happy.' Her hand closed over his. 'Very happy.'

He drove on, thinking: *Once the baby's born and the paper's published, I can find a decent job somewhere ...*

Amina, who knew that Dr Crowe wouldn't allow Harry's name on the paper under any circumstances, and probably wouldn't even give him a decent reference, looked at him and thought: *How can I keep him happy? How can I do what's best for our child?* Inside her, the baby kicked.

This Large Print Book for the Partially sighted, who cannot read normal print, is published under the auspices of

THE ULVERSCROFT FOUNDATION

THE ULVERSCROFT FOUNDATION

. . . we hope that you have enjoyed this Large Print Book. Please think for a moment about those people who have worse eyesight problems than you . . . and are unable to even read or enjoy Large Print, without great difficulty.

You can help them by sending a donation, large or small to:

The Ulverscroft Foundation, 1, The Green, Bradgate Road, Anstey, Leicestershire, LE7 7FU, England.
or request a copy of our brochure for more details.

The Foundation will use all your help to assist those people who are handicapped by various sight problems and need special attention.

Thank you very much for your help.